DECEPTIVE DIME STORE DEMONS

A Flea Market Magic Novel

NEW YORK TIMES BESTSELLING AUTHOR

SHAWNTELLE MADISON

VALKYRIE RISING PRESS

eBook ISBN: 978-1-7344510-2-3

Print ISBN: 978-1-7344510-3-0

Natalya Christmas Artwork Copyright: Kate Sherron

Heart and Pile of Ornaments Artwork Copyright: RC

Editing by: MK Books Editing, Editing720

www.valkyrierisingpress.com

"All the world needs is more donuts," my best friend Aggie told me as we headed up the stairwell to her new apartment. "There's something for everyone. Bear claws, cream-filled, gluten-free, and those *pyshki* ones your mom bakes."

I wrinkled my nose as Aggie cradled a sack of groceries in one hand and a box of donuts in the other.

If only those custard-filled, happiness-in-a-bite confectionaries had such power. Donuts were notorious for being gooey, germ-laden morsels or rock-hard lint traps.

"Just you wait." She adjusted her goodies. "I heard that Bashful Brownies Baking Company has a new selection of enchanted cake donuts. Just one nibble and you'll forget carbs or calories even existed."

I balanced the boxes in my arms and kept smiling. If one of those donuts could magically haul her stuff up these stairs, I'd be game. "Where did you find the furniture for the place?" I asked.

"Actually, like the humans, I used my persuasive personality to get a deal at Furniture Mart."

"That's good." We made it up yet another flight of steps before I said what was truly on my mind.

"How come you don't want to live in my old house?" I said, only a little hurt. "Is it the plastic bins I store there?"

Aggie never minded my collecting—well, hoarding habits —before. Just mentioning my stuff brought the tidy rows of packed away holiday cheer to mind and shame followed.

She carried the bag of groceries up the steps, and I hurried behind her. "You know it's not that. I need a fresh start. Your old house has got too many memories of *him*."

I sighed, knowing by *him* she meant Will, her former boyfriend. Aggie had returned to South Toms River a couple of weeks ago, then her ex-husband had kidnapped her. Will swooped in, kicked some ass, and rescued her. I still hadn't asked Aggie about what had happened the night Will had saved her, but that conversation would happen sooner or later.

Maybe a pizza, donuts, and ice cream night at Aggie's new place would lighten her mood.

We finally made it to Aggie's new apartment on the fourth floor. I dropped my box off to the side and sucked in the cool air. June had come to a roaring end this past weekend, and now we were into the first week of July. This month promised sweaty armpits, incessant mosquitos, and burnt toes on pavement. A delightful summer, I say.

I swept my gaze over Aggie's home. She had a top floor studio apartment with a bunch of nice perks: skylights, an open floor plan, oak floors, and a fresh coat of white paint. (Give me the clean slate of a painted wall any day.) The faint scent of cigarette smoke lingered near the balcony, but other than that, I liked the place.

While Aggie hefted sacks of groceries onto the kitchen island, I couldn't help but ask, "So is there a reason you're in the same apartment building as Erica?"

Aggie snorted. "South Toms River is a *tiny* town even for New Jersey. The selection left little to be desired."

With the hum that only a mother carrying her children would make, Aggie stuffed four to five servings of food into her fridge. I held in a laugh. I didn't bother griping about her overeating habit, and she supported me while I worked through my obsessive-compulsive disorder.

"Does she know you're moving in?" I asked.

"She'll know when she comes home from work." Aggie winked at me.

I gave her a wary look.

"Chill, Nat, chill. People change. Erica might be ready to change, too."

"Maybe."

"Are you worried Erica and I are going to become BFFs? Maybe we'll polish our nails and binge Netflix variety shows?"

That got a laugh out of me. "That doesn't sound like your kind of thing."

"Maybe not now, but who knows? You really need to learn how to trust others."

I rolled my eyes.

"Yes," Aggie admitted, "she tried to force Thorn to marry her."

My eyebrow rose at the mention of my husband, and I waited for her to keep going.

"And she mocked you five ways from Sunday."

I folded my arms. Might as well accept the reminders and let them bounce off.

"But in the end, you came out top dog." She tapped my shoulder. "You're alpha female and you have Thorn. It's time for you to move on. Make peace with those who have wronged you."

I snorted. She had a point, but what could you do when a

shit-ton of people pissed in your backyard, walked away with a middle-finger salute, and then you're stuck in the aftermath?

Speaking of hands… "Have you ever painted your nails?" I asked.

She opened a bag of dill pickle chips and tossed one into her mouth. "When I got married," she said dryly. "So, when do you have to report in at the demon's store?"

"Don't remind me. I can't believe I got myself into this mess." Back when the Basilisk King wreaked havoc on the town, I broke into a rival flea market to buy—yes, I broke in and left money—an item crucial to uncovering who was behind the attacks. In the process, I angered the flea market's owner, a goblin named Kramkar, and I became indebted to him for a favor: a limited employment agreement.

But that wasn't the fun part.

I learned I wouldn't work at Kramkar's store; he made another deal and hurled me toward *another* store. Good God, these supernatural creatures tossed around deals like Halloween candy.

I glanced at my watch. "T-minus six hours until I have to show up. This is my first job at a twenty-four-hour shop."

Aggie's reddish-blonde eyebrows rose. "Feeding the shopaholics all night long, huh? Sounds like the perfect place for you."

"The prospects of getting my shop-freak on whenever I want sounds divine, but I'm not so sure about demons. Have you ever met one?"

"Probably. A lot of the ladies I've met on the Upper East Side are probably demons. They raise hell if little Johnny or Jenny don't get into one of those upper-crusty boarding schools." She offered me a chip, but I passed. "Look, the Basilisk King isn't a threat anymore. Just put on your big-girl panties, march on in there, and sell some shit."

All that sounded easier said than done. Less than a month ago, Thorn had left town for a conference. Not long into his absence, all hell broke loose as mysterious trunks showed up around town. My friends and I learned that the trunk hoarder, the Basilisk King, was a part of a magical shift happening. The Great Northern Fairy Path shifted southward and brought magical mayhem of epic proportions to our doorstep.

Even with the Basilisk King gone, I'd learned the hard way that when you think you've cleaned the dog shit off your shoe, there are more piles out there to step in.

At least all I had to do was work at another supernatural store for a while. A week should be easy-peasy.

"You've faced some pretty crazy shit," Aggie said with her mouth full. "I'm betting you'll either make some extra cash on the side, or you'll buy half their stock."

I flashed her an *I-doubt-it* look. As tempting as shiny, holiday-oriented treats could be, many of them might be possessed or something. The last thing I needed was a haunted pair of Christmas shears cutting holes through my *Santa Loves Me* sweaters.

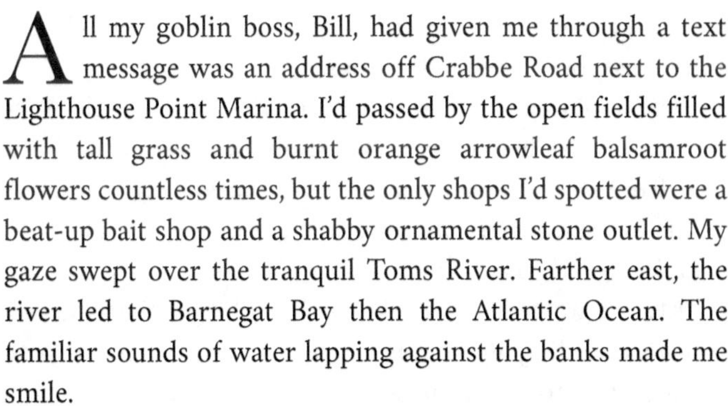

All my goblin boss, Bill, had given me through a text message was an address off Crabbe Road next to the Lighthouse Point Marina. I'd passed by the open fields filled with tall grass and burnt orange arrowleaf balsamroot flowers countless times, but the only shops I'd spotted were a beat-up bait shop and a shabby ornamental stone outlet. My gaze swept over the tranquil Toms River. Farther east, the river led to Barnegat Bay then the Atlantic Ocean. The familiar sounds of water lapping against the banks made me smile.

My home is a beautiful place.

Back when I was a kid, my dad and uncles often took my brother, Alex, and me on fishing trips. Uncle Boris loved fishing trips on the Toms River. We never caught anything—Uncle Boris was too busy talking his head off. He'd sit there with a half-inch lit cigarette dangling from one hand and a beat-up fishing pole in the other. His advice about life, women, and buying a trust-worthy truck made little sense, but our time with him left feel-good memories of sunshine, rampant bug bites, and laughter.

Time to check out the stone and ornament outlet.

From the outside, the store looked like any other. In front, the place had stone ornaments like lawn gnomes, fawns, ornate pagodas and even an elaborately carved dragon or two. A chain-link fence surrounded the more expensive items like marble slabs or cut sandstone for pathways and landscaping. But none of those things interested me. What I needed to find was the entrance and determine what I'd face today.

So far nothing smelled amiss here. Matter of fact, the wind carried the decadent scents from the nearby Bashful Brownie Baking Company.

This late in the day, I expected fewer customers in the parking lot. At least a dozen cars, from a rundown-looking Chevy to five pricey-looking Town and Country vehicles, filled the spots closest to the door.

The building itself was nondescript. The single-story brick structure had a few rectangular windows in the front. The front door was left ajar, perhaps beckoning customers inside to see what treasures they'd uncover.

I don't mind if I do.

After I walked across the parking lot to the concrete sidewalk leading up to the store, I hurried along a path lined with stone carvings of nymphs and seahorses. I wondered why the owners protected the marble, yet their fencing didn't surround the figurines and statues in front. Maybe they had enchantments to keep happy thief fingers at bay.

As I passed the stone carvings their imperfections smacked me in the face. Michelangelo wasn't making these goods. Moss grew here and there while some had hideous designs with misshapen mouths and body parts in the wrong places. But the worst travesty of them all: tiny chips—though minuscule to the human eye—marred much of the merchandise.

I shook my head. From the mouth of one cheap goblin boss into the hands of cheap demons.

On the way inside, I walked by a human couple. The woman clutched a sales receipt and she gabbed with her companion about how excited grandma would be once they added lawn gnomes to her bed of daisies and tulips.

Hopefully, they don't plan to purchase anything from the front, I thought.

Based on the narrow front-end, I assumed I'd find a tiny store, but to my delight, the establishment stretched toward the river for at least one hundred feet or so. What smelled like humans, with their pockets lined with dirty cash, browsed shelves of ceramics along the walls and four rows along the center.

With raised eyebrows, I assessed the goods. A peculiar odor like fermented fruit dashed around displays with teapots. To my right, mugs with garish purple, pink, and puke green designs that screamed *I break easily* sat next to a hodgepodge of products like ceramic thimbles, clocks, and planters. If a potter could craft a mold, these folks stocked it. God help me if I spotted a ceramic codpiece.

A rather short clerk wearing a maroon apron around her waist approached me. Her dark-brown hair softly framed a small cherubic face. The woman's red T-shirt boldly claimed she was a cat-lady-in-training.

"Excuse me?" I asked. "I'm part of the evening staff for a couple days."

Confusion added a blush to her freckled cheeks. "Well, that's news to me." She quirked a frown. "As usual."

"I don't understand."

She extended her hand. "I'm Dayla, the daytime manager. I don't know much about your shift, but feel free to head to the back office. Mimi, the night manager, is working outside."

Through the windows, the sun finally set. As if right on cue, the customers ended their conversation, and with zombie-like precision, they left the store. One short woman even gently put down the vase she examined and marched outside.

I turned around to ask Dayla what happened, and she'd vanished too.

Was it something I said?

A minute passed. The only movement came from a newspaper sailing across the road through the window. The dead quiet settled into my soul. Wow, that felt nice.

My mini vacation ended as quickly as it started. The front door opened, and a new set of customers streamed inside. Fairies hidden under glamours, or spells that mask their true appearance, grabbed carts and browsed. Now fairies come in all shapes and sizes from small brownies that resemble little children to elves that vary by skin color and height. The fairy folk in this store dressed like tourists from all walks of life.

Over the years, I'd encountered all kinds of supernatural creatures. Many of them had malicious intentions. Seeing their true nature as a mystical goods antiquarian was key. Through Bill's enchantments, I could see through their glamours, and therefore, I had an idea what kind of bullshit I'd encounter.

I wandered through the store, even stopping by the register to snag an apron the last clerk had left behind.

Thanks for the latte stain on the front, Dayla.

I needed to break in a fresh spray-and-wash pen, anyway.

While I attacked the stain with my trusty tool, a brownie approached the counter to buy a teapot. The register from the late 2000s wouldn't earn the owners any points, but I knew what to do—until a cold woman's hand touched mine. I turned with a growl to see a towering, hooded figure. I couldn't make out who lurked underneath the rough cloth garment. Only that she stank of ozone that came after a thunderstorm. With a bump of her hard hip, she shoved me out of the way.

"Go see Mademoiselle Midnight, Wolf." With one deathly pale hand, she pointed to the rear doorway, while with the other she completed the transaction.

Might as well follow instructions. I ventured to the so-called back office, but the cracked-open doorway's new location made little sense. I distinctly remembered the door sat near the northwest corner. Now it was on the other side.

As a natural-born werewolf, I shouldn't blink twice about this type of thing. Didn't I shapeshift during the full moon? Hadn't I spent my childhood having sleepovers with fairies? But the hairs on the back of my head stood on end. A new scent crossed my nose.

Was that pumpkin spice?

I followed the scent toward the new doorway, but I took my time. After all the adventures I'd experienced, especially with a goblin boss like Bill, I needed to protect myself.

Beyond the exit, I didn't find an office but a short hallway leading outside. A grassy path led to a dock out to the river. I expected to see lights from homes and businesses dotting the opposite bank, but I had a far crazier view. At the end of the pier sat a late-twentieth-century, two-story paddleboat. Damn, it was beautiful. I'd learned about them during a history course back in college. Thin lines of smoke rose from a double chimney, while lanterns scattered along the second-story iron railing cast an eerie burnt-orange glow.

The rough wood yawned as I made my way down the dock. Fireflies in my path darted out of the way. The pumpkin-like scent strengthened as I drew closer.

A ramp at the boat's bow provided passage to the Main Deck. Before I could venture inside, a woman materialized in front of me.

"You must be my new clerk." The woman, with tightly coiled, chartreuse hair and skin a rich shade of almond, stood no taller than my shoulder. Strange, tiny lights sparkled in her hair. She pursed her full lips and assessed me with half-closed lids. I shivered. My new employer wore a long black peplum top and midnight-blue leather skirt. Her feet were bare. The wind off the river tugged at the trail bottom of her top, but I couldn't see the end, only that it disappeared like the smoke off the chimney.

"I am." I added strength to my voice. "I'm Natalya Stravinsky. I was told to report here."

She flicked her fingers to beckon me to follow. We walked down the Main Deck, passing open doorways into the first floor's interior. I peeked through each door to find more eclectic inventory, like ceramic pipes and delicate carved birds, stored in glass displays. "I'm Mademoiselle Midnight, and the VIP section of my storefront is called the Midnight Barge."

"Looks nice." I appreciated anything shiny.

"The goblin told me you're *too* efficient and I'd be in great hands, but..."

"But?"

"I don't trust men or monsters."

I gave her a nod thinking of Aggie's words. "Trust should be earned."

She strode past a shimmering terracotta ladle lying in the middle of a red velvet pillow. Vivid depictions of a Greek battle on the side caught my eye. "The Daylight Dame and I are new to town, but I'm not new to selling. A couple of months ago, I paid a large sum to buy this shop from a human to capitalize on the supernatural traffic She Who Always Walks the Path brings."

Lovely, another opportunist. My sister-in-law Karey, along with her aunt, Mevelyn, had warned me about them.

"Her path hasn't changed for the last two thousand years," Mevelyn had said. *"We must know if other powerful beings are proceeding her. Those leeches are dangerous."*

Just thinking about the wood nymph pushed me to a dark place I didn't want to be, so I focused on my new boss. I'd think about what happened between Mevelyn and me on another day.

Finally, we reached the steamboat's stern. More glass displays and pedestals with ceramic rare goods formed a U-shape in this open area. Beyond that, the paddle wheel sat silent. All around us, translucent figures shifted from one item to another. I squinted and waited for Bill's enchantment to kick in, but these wisps of smoke and light either had no true form or I'd encountered something new.

One murky gray apparition swept past me. When it brushed against my shoulder, icy shards nipped at my skin.

That was never a good thing.

Focus on the job, Natalya, I reminded myself.

I switched to familiarizing myself with the Main Deck layout. A set of stairs to my right descended into dark waters, while another set led to the Hurricane Deck above.

"What's down there?" I could've asked how come the magical ship hadn't sunk yet, but why bother?

"There's a submerged floor below the Main Deck for water spirits, but since you can't hold your breath…we'll let that area go for now." The way she eyed me while she added "for now" meant I might need to sprout gills this week.

"And upstairs?"

"Off-limits. You have no business roaming around the Boiler or Hurricane Decks."

Fine by me. Less madness to manage.

Mademoiselle Midnight ended my tour with an introduction to the ancient embossed copper cash register nearby. Her fingers caressed the large black buttons ranging from NO SALE up to fifty dollars, and the machine clicked in response. I admired the ornate fleur-de-lis and delicate swirls along the top and sides. A polished mahogany base glinted from a nearby railing lantern.

"Pay attention, Naomi," she said sternly. "I only want to show you once."

I opened my mouth to correct her, but shut my trap while she flew through the sequence of processing a purchase.

Read the price tag.

Say the price, no negotiation. No, really—none.

Click the appropriate button. Wait for the ding.

Package the item in one of the black boxes stacked near the paddle wheel.

Seemed easy enough.

I filed the instructions away in the Vault of Job Satisfaction. Now that I knew what I needed to do, I decided to do a sweep along the Main Deck, but my manager blocked my passage.

"One more thing, Nancy." Her smile stretched to unnatural lengths. "My dearest sister, Dayla, fought me at every step to come here. My success hinges on profits and perfor-mance. If you interfere with my plans, I'll *eat* you."

My breath caught. "Excuse me?"

The relaxed features on her delicate face spoke volumes. She was dead serious. Her softened expression slipped into a honey-warm smile as she glanced around me to peer at the dock.

"We have distinguished customers arriving," she whispered. "Greet them well, Nina."

I opened my mouth to correct her yet again but then shrugged. I had to do my job well first, then figure out how to get through this agreement without ending up as her supper.

Two lines of ten fairies followed a single one. The ladies strolled up the ramp and joined us. The fairy in front wore garments boasting of her station and wealth. While her companions were in light blue summer dresses, she was dressed in a tailored A-line dress with a pink cardigan. Her skin glistened as if dew formed along her neckline. A single poppy adorned her pinned-up black hair. They all smelled of lilies about to bloom and spring rain after a downpour.

When she passed us, my employer gave her a curt nod and I did the same.

"Good evening, Lady Ophelia," Mademoiselle Midnight said. "What a pleasant surprise to have a member from the Spring Court visit my store. May I help you find anything this evening?"

Lady Ophelia sniffed. "Just browsing through your rare goods before the Summer Court soils your boat with their stench."

My manager gestured for the lady and her entourage to explore. When I didn't move to join them, the demon jerked her chin their way.

Jeez. Did she think they planned to steal something? I had

yet to learn about the merchandise. How could I help anyone? While I scurried to accompany them through the first room, I scanned each product sign below their respective displays.

Cracked Pan's Flute, read one.

Queen Me'Hitan's Pleasure Pipe, read another.

I didn't want to see what *that* was and hurried to catch up.

Right off the first room, Lady Ophelia stopped here and there, but I'd seen shoppers like her before. They glanced about as if they didn't care—but I fixed my gaze on Lady Ophelia's light gray eyes. She'd lingered in front of a set of arrowhead clay molds, even sidled toward the center display with two urns circling each other. With each stop, her eyes flitted to a simple whistle resting on a crimson silk pillow. It was lovely and had a tiny pawprint on the side.

From across the room, I read the Russian script.

"*Cobachee Svistok Tserbera*," I whispered.

Why did she want Cerberus's Dog Whistle? Calling a three-headed hellhound *never* sounded like a good idea. I'd rather unleash Uncle Boris's God-awful cologne on the masses. Maybe the whistle had other uses.

"My lady, is there anything you'd like to see?" I inched toward her. "The *svistok*, perhaps?"

She sniffed again, and her ladies-in-waiting parted for her to see me.

"It looks beautiful." As her grin grew, her floral aroma switched from lilies to fragrant roses. "Could I hold it—"

"The whistle isn't for sale," Mademoiselle Midnight said from behind me. Her pumpkin spice scent flared shortly after.

Damn, having these creatures sneak around me would murder my anxiety. I glanced over my shoulder to see my employer right outside the exit.

The fairy's smile wilted. "Then why have it out in the open to tempt your patrons, Ms. Midnight?"

"Oh, it's for sale," the night demon said smoothly. "But not for you."

Surprise briefly touched the attendants' faces as Lady Ophelia's shoulders stiffened. "I'll pay double."

"No." The night demon folded her arms.

Lady Ophelia drew a deep breath before she spoke. "My court is spending the season in Manhattan. Not long after we arrived, a predator made its presence known."

"Is it hunting you through the aisles of Saks Fifth Ave?" Mademoiselle Midnight's dark eyes flashed with amusement.

"New York City can be as deadly as the Old Lands," Lady Ophelia said. "No matter the danger, I refuse to die without striking back first."

The night demon chuffed. "Why bother? Return to the Old Lands."

"And sit in the heat with those stuffy bitches from the Summer Court? Or maybe we should bow before the autumn ladies or watch the Winter Court wither away?" Lady Ophelia's soft smile veered to a sneer. "I prefer the fragile humans and their simple pleasures."

The spring fairy glanced at me as if she expected me to intervene. "I'm the customer. You can't speak on my behalf?"

"I'm sorry, my lady," I said. "The management has the final say."

The searing glare she threw at me could've burnt a rack of lamb. I'd met many frightening fairies before, but I'd never encountered a high-ranking, disgruntled fairy customer.

With a turn of her heel, Lady Ophelia escaped through another exit. Her entourage stomped after her.

Seeing a customer's retreating back rarely bothered me. She wouldn't be the first or the *last* pissed-off patron. I observed her departure to the dock with a healthy space between us. Normally I didn't care—hadn't she said the problem was in New York? That was an hour and a half away. Just over fifty beautiful miles of space. And yet, I knew based on past experiences that distance didn't matter when weird shit always found a way to my doorstep.

Mademoiselle Midnight materialized again right next to me. I was ready this time. She stiffly lit a half-used cigarette.

"Guess she won't be signing up for our Frequent Buyer Program." She drew in a deep drag, but she never exhaled the smoke.

"You ever encountered a pissed-off fairy, Natalie?" she added. "I'd be careful. The courts hold grudges like no other."

CHAPTER 2

My long night stretched out like a half-moon during its seemingly endless march across the sky. Above my head, the cloudless heavens shifted from black to dark purple. The twinkling stars flashed me a few winks, and soon, the sun hinted its arrival on the lavender-tinted horizon.

The ominous and silent spirits left me wide-eyed and confused most of the time. It took me five or six times of stumbling through customer service to figure things out. Some of the spirit customers carried their selections—not sure how they did it, to be honest—while others waited next to what they wanted. They paid using the silver flecks of light that floated to the cash register.

As I completed a final sweep of the Main Deck, the customers scattered like ash from a firepit. I murmured my thanks, but without body language or speech, I had no idea whether they returned the gesture or flipped me off.

Once every customer departed, I searched for Mademoiselle Midnight. Might as well give her my thoughts—but lo-

and-behold, my new boss had made a run for it, too. Even an ominous fog appeared around the boat. Maybe that was a sign I should jump ship? I hurried down the ramp to the dock and didn't look back until I reached my car in the parking lot.

This whole place had the timing of a perfectly prepared pot roast.

As I'd sensed, the Midnight Barge melted away into the thickening gloom while a car or two pulled into the store's parking lot to wait for its opening. I chuckled. Just like at The Bends, eager humans came early to snatch up the shiny stuff.

Time to go home and get some much needed rest.

Once I reached the Parkway, I rolled down the window to let the rising sun tickle my face. Instead, the rising stench of something burning swatted me on the nose. I scanned the horizon and spotted a thickening plume to the southwest. Forest fires struck the town once in a while. With Jake Branch County Park and Double Trouble State Park to the south and more nature preserves to the north and west, the area had a high chance of brush fires.

As hard as I tried to ignore the fire, a cold sweat slammed into my back and stole my breath. The rational part of me—which I'd worked diligently to let run my life—cried a horrid death as a singular question hit: did that fire originate at the home I shared with Thorn? It could be from our house, but as I drove deeper into the woods, I had an idea the minute I passed the turnoff to my cottage.

My home was fine, but Grantham cabin lay ahead.

And the moment Thorn might've smelled the smoke from our house, he would've checked on his father and younger brother, Will.

I picked up the phone, grateful for speed-dial as my insides quaked. The line rang and rang.

"C'mon, Thorn. This is where you pick up and tell me, 'Everything's fine, babe.'"

When the call jumped to his answering service, I was proud of myself for catching my breath and somewhat calmly saying, "Hey, you. Will you call me back? I saw a fire near Farley's place."

The thickening scent of charred wood and brush threatened to wrap around my throat. The shrill wails from the firetrucks strengthened. Trees whipped past me, blending in a dark smear as I focused on the road.

I turned down the winding path to the cabin and met the line of firetrucks from not only the local firehouse but also Ocean County.

Not good.

My heartbeat roared louder and louder as emergency vehicle traffic forced me to the side of the road. I abandoned my Nissan, discarded my low heels, and sprinted through the trees, pantyhose be damned.

The flashing lights from the firetrucks bled through the tall pines as I approached the clearing to the Grantham cabin. During sunrise, this home had an imposing presence. Dawn's light usually cast a haunting glow on the windows and the dark wooden columns along the front. The second story windows reminded me of a fire-breathing dragon that waited with outstretched arms.

But now that a cloud of smoke and fire engulfed the cabin, I stopped cold to gasp.

What the hell happened?

A year ago, back when Farley was pack leader, I'd entered this house with trepidation as I'd asked Farley to re-enter the pack that had shunned me. In my mind, I could still see the foyer I'd traipsed through with Farley waiting in a La-Z-Boy chair with his feet propped up.

He had harsh words for me that fateful day.

"I've seen your place," he'd said to me while his westerns blared on his big screen TV. "And I've seen you around town. You would be a liability."

According to the Code, or the rules werewolves used to govern themselves, flawed werewolves like me represented a weakened link in the chain.

Even knowing those rules, I tried and succeeded in re-entering the pack.

I darted around firemen and policemen, waiting for my nose to tell my heart that everything was fine. That I might find my mate standing behind those soot-covered faces and men in uniform. A few cops recognized me and called out my name, but I didn't pause until I caught Thorn's scent. His dark blue SUV sat next to his brother's beat-up sedan. I circled the cars twice and followed the trail.

I raced around to the back of the smoking ruins where I encountered three men huddled together. Each of the Grantham men reflected moments in time. Thorn's younger brother, Will, crouched on the ground, his eyes glazed over. My mate stood to the far right. His filthy, blond hair stuck to his scalp and his eyes formed slits as he stared at what was left of the house. Between the Grantham boys stood their father, Farley. His blond hair darkened over his ears where gray hairs sprouted. Every time I saw him, I caught glimpses of Thorn in the Grantham patriarch from Thorn's strong chin to his broad shoulders, but Thorn's face more closely resembled his mother, Pearl, who'd passed away when we were kids. As I approached them, the Grantham family patriarch didn't stare at the house.

He glared at me.

How dare she come here, his eyes conveyed.

How dare she witness this moment of vulnerability? his sneer implied.

My gaze crashed to the ground. I hurried to my mate.

"Thorn." He wrapped his arms around me. Absolute relief washed over me as he kissed the top of my head. "Why didn't you answer your phone?"

He reached into his pocket and pulled out a dead phone with a cracked screen.

"I sent a smoke signal instead," he said with a sigh.

"Not funny."

"No direction to go but up right now." His voice was hoarse.

I drew my nose across the crook of his neck. Underneath the stench of burnt wood, his scent lingered. I murmured a prayer of thanks.

Time passed as the sun rose higher in the sky. Cops and firemen chatted with Thorn and Farley. I waited off to the side. After working all night, I should've fallen into a stupor, but my senses jumped all over the place. The wet mud chilled the bottom of my feet while acrid soot coated my tongue and left my empty stomach soured. Sweat gathered on my palms, and I feared the bacteria frolicking between my fingers.

Soon enough, we returned to Thorn's SUV. My father-in-law hadn't spoken a single word to me. Words of consolation formed in my mouth, but I didn't know how to convey that I'd do everything in my power to help. Would he even care?

"I'll take Dad and Will to the house," Thorn said. "Are you coming straight home?"

"Let's ride together and I'll pick up my car later," I offered.

Thorn slowly nodded.

Farley got in the passenger side backseat while I waited for Thorn and Will to wrap up a quick conversation with the cops. The morning light hit the top of the car, but shadows prevailed around the former pack leader.

My father-in-law sat slumped forward. Smudges marked

the endless wrinkles along his bitter face. His hard glower into the woods made me wonder if he stared down a hidden enemy or had decided to start a war with the inevitability of time.

CHAPTER 3

During the somber drive to the cottage I shared with my mate, a dark cowl blanketed the vehicle. My stomach clenched tighter as my quaint home grew larger in the view. What should've been my sanctuary with my husband loomed between the protective groves of thick pine and elm trees.

Even the beds of golden sunflowers and fragrant chrysanthemums I planted in the front yard drooped over from the Jersey heat. Usually, I watered them when I got home from The Bends, but today my new work schedule had shoved my routine into the disorganization bin.

I glanced at Thorn in the driver's seat as he parked next to the cottage. His usual happy-go-lucky expression had vanished. He grasped my left hand and squeezed it gently. I waited for him to let me go, but he held on for two or three breaths as Will and Farley got out of the back. Farley was empty-handed, while Will held a covered plastic tub with what little they had salvaged before the fire grew too large.

Farley limped up to the house. I watched his retreating back, wondering how his old knee injury fared. Many years ago, back when Farley was pack leader, a rival had challenged the miserable man to become alpha over the South Toms River Pack and nearly won. Farley's knee injury hadn't healed well, and after that, old age had caught up with him.

Even with a limp, Farley didn't wait for us, so I hurried after them. How I wished I had a spell to teleport them to the local Holiday Inn, but even I knew that wouldn't solve the underlying problem. Their home had burned to the ground, and a week with a free continental breakfast wouldn't bring them a new home any sooner.

Nor would it help their meager bank account.

Working class men like the Granthams didn't have a hoard of cash. After Thorn graduated from college, he ended up working in the business office at the local mill. I had yet to see Farley work a day in my life. And right after Will left high school, he attended community college for a while, but eventually he jumped from one menial job to another.

Briefly, I considered the house I used to live in, standing empty on the other side of town. I still stored a couple of boxes there too. The very idea of having a man like him soil my sanctuary soured my stomach, but it might be the only solution in the long run.

But would Farley even want to be in my debt? Especially after he walked into the cottage.

Farley took his time after Thorn opened the door. I bit my lower lip as anxiety crept up my spine and sank its teeth into the nape of my neck. I hesitated to follow, lingering on the front porch to avoid seeing Farley's reaction. Thorn's younger brother had seen my hidden shame many times before. Will walked into the living room and slumped onto the couch, not once taking note of the plastic tubs containing my hoard of holiday cheer. Usually when I returned home, these things—the holiday sweaters, sparkly tree ornaments, and plastic-wrapped nutcrackers—gave me unadulterated joy. These precious baubles represented memories of a life with a family that gathered and cared for one another.

But as Farley's stern blue eyes swept over the stacks containing 424 ornaments and doodads, the crushing sensation in my neck deepened enough to take my breath away.

Within my haze, I caught Farley's dry mumble.

"Where can I sit?" Not once did he look away from my collection.

There were plenty of seats in the living room, from the sofa to the armchair in the corner. The single La-Z-Boy had a set of holiday cookbooks in front of it. Thorn picked up the books and gestured toward the chair.

"Sit there, Dad." Thorn disappeared into the kitchen. He didn't have to tell me where he'd put the cookbooks; I caught his soft footsteps as he stowed them away in our small kitchen pantry.

I had yet to let my little friends into that room out of consideration for Thorn.

I hadn't realized I stood at the edge of the living room and foyer until Will said, "I feel gross. You want a shower first, Dad?"

I could feel the burn of Grandma Lasovskaya scolding me for not making my guests feel welcome. "What kind of Stravinsky *devushka* are you?" she'd say. "Didn't I teach you to be a good girl? When someone—especially your kin—arrives, you must feed them."

Yes, my mother, who cooked and burned meat like the best of them, would've already had lamb or a roast chopped and simmering in the pot.

But my feet remained rooted to the spot while the Grantham men spoke.

"I don't care." Farley scratched through his shaggy, blond hair. Bits of dirt rained down on the floor. My heart rate picked up and something inside me, perhaps the rational part, forced me to suck in a deep breath.

Put on your big-girl pastel panties and wake up, Nat.

I knew damn well it would be rude to ask either of them to sit on a blanket. I resigned myself to clean later. Hell, I'd worked all night. Why not spend an hour or two cleaning up my house?

Thorn entered the living room, and I jumped into manager mode. "Why don't you find them some clothes to wear and work out a schedule for showers while I make some breakfast?"

"A schedule for showers? Really?" With a sigh, Thorn nodded.

I tried to smile. I really did. I suspected my clown-like attempt hadn't worked when Thorn took my hand again and squeezed. He kissed the top of my head and lingered until my faltering heart skipped a beat.

Hello, Earth, I think I'm back home.

I hurried into the kitchen, shoving away thoughts of who'd sleep where. What little messes they'd leave behind. What objects they'd push here or there.

My therapist Dr. Frank had given me tools over our various therapy sessions for how to cope with anxiety and situations that grew out of my control, but right now I couldn't set my derailed mind back on track.

I straightened my back and gathered the materials to make southwest egg muffin cups. I even turned on the radio on top of the microwave to the local jazz station. Lining up the seasonings, fresh eggs, onions, chiles, and bell peppers on the counter drew me to a happy place. In that warm pool of relaxation, the anxious human jumped aside while the wolf within did what needed to be done.

Procure food for the pack.

Duke Ellington and his band's lively songs from his

Newport Festival Suite filled the kitchen with piano, drums, and saucy trumpets. The rise and fall of the horn section made my head bob while the shower turned on in the bathroom. What better way to pass the time and forget about your troubles than amid the magic of musical notes? The morning sun rose higher as I mixed the ingredients, but even Duke Ellington's sway over me waned as anxiousness seeped from my pores.

I startled when Thorn wrapped his arms around my waist and pressed my back against his chest.

"You're okay," he whispered. "We're okay."

I closed my eyes and tried to let him steady me like he always did. Wouldn't he need comfort right now too?

Words I wanted to say tasted like cayenne pepper on my tongue. Each one would grow hotter and hotter until I boiled within. I merely nodded instead of saying what I needed to say. What I needed to feel. I didn't want reminders of how Farley perceived me, but then again, I couldn't control him.

I could only control myself. And that would have to be enough for now.

With the southwest eggs bubbling in the muffin container in the oven, I tidied the kitchen then escaped to my bedroom. The warmth of the blue walls and the soft cotton comforter on my bed soothed me. If I didn't have breakfast in the oven, I would've burrowed into my blankets and turned myself into a Natalya burrito. Even the daylight peeking behind my curtains wouldn't keep me from clocking out. My shoulders sagged and the events from last night circled through my head.

The dark flashes of anger from the fairy, who looked like she just got off the plane from a shopping trip to Monte Carlo, wouldn't have scared most folks. A brisk wind would've blown her over, but I'd tangled with fairies before. A year ago, I'd learned my dad had a moon debt—a werewolf's debt to another werewolf. Circumstances arose where I had to help, and in the process, I'd encountered a family of dangerous spring fairies, in particular, a little girl named Lisbetta. On the outside, she exuded innocence with her angelic face and tiny frame, but that had all been a facade for the predator under the skin. The tiny spring fairy queen had peculiar powers, including a frightening gift of draining the essence from other creatures.

I shuddered and made a mental note: don't fuck with fairies.

Twenty minutes later, the alarm on my phone dinged. Time to fetch the eggs and get the meal on the table. As much as I tried not to eat outside of the kitchen without protective measures in place to keep everything tidy, I decided to grab a plate and stuff my face in my bedroom. The boys could eat when they felt like it.

Of course, my master plan turned into an epic failure when I walked into the kitchen to find the four-seater table set. All three Grantham men sat there, waiting, as ominous as the Three Fates. While the food had cooked, my handy mate had set the table, added toasted bagels and even cut apples into slices. Damn, he'd even perfectly lined up the forks and spoons under paper napkins.

I edged toward them. Farley chewed on a bagel and didn't look at me. Will shoveled the eggs into his mouth like he hadn't seen a meal in years.

"Thanks for the food, Nat," Will said between bites.

I hammered a smile onto my face. "Glad you like them. A customer of mine shared the recipe a couple years ago."

"They're really good," Thorn added. "I'd like to learn the recipe."

I settled in the only remaining seat—the one right across from Farley. It's amazing that four feet from someone could feel like four inches. Almost as if his distant expression was pressed against my chest, weighing heavy and dark.

To release his hold over me, I got up to wash my hands. Not once but twice. An old habit I thought I'd tamed.

When I returned to the table, I sensed Farley's stern reproach.

Thorn ended the silence. "You both need clothes, right? We can buy some shirts after you work today."

"Sounds good," Will replied. "I got called into work, but I'm taking the day off—"

"Again?" Farley snapped. "Why? That's at least a full day's wages." He slowly shook his head. "Young folks these days always needin' a day off if their *feelings* are hurt."

Will stiffened then gulped down the rest of his orange juice.

"He just lost all his belongings, Dad." Thorn's deep voice added calm to the room. "Give him a break."

"The electric company and all them other folks won't give us a break at the end of the month," Farley griped.

Will's jaw twitched with irritation. "What can they do to us? Turn off the water?"

Farley slowly ate an apple slice and avoided the serving of southwest eggs on his plate. "You might have shitty credit, boy, after running off for some woman, but I plan to use mine to get a better place...somehow."

That word *somehow* blossomed into a stink. Long ago, the pack had accrued debts. Many of those debts had been paid, but now the Granthams' only assets lay in their land and their position as the alpha in the South Toms River Pack.

As much as I wanted to chime in, as a member of the pack, it felt like I was intruding on a family affair.

Damn shame I couldn't contribute since I'd married into that family.

Farley opened his mouth to spew more nonsense about Will calling his boss when a heavy knock hit the front door.

"Who's that?" Will asked.

"I'll get it." I needed the space. By the time I reached the doorway, I could smell our visitors, and my heart lifted when I opened the door to see my mom and Aunt Vera. The Stravinsky women didn't wait for me to greet them. They kissed my cheek and bounded into the house with a hot Crock-Pot and covered casserole bowl in hand. How they'd prepared them that quickly didn't matter. The Stravinskys always had spare food.

"I heard what happened from your uncle," Aunt Vera said in Russian as she floated away from me. "So terrible! I called your mama, and we came here to check on them."

The Stravinsky women entered the kitchen as if they owned the place. Aunt Vera took over my seat and happily placed the casserole dish in the center of the table. She removed the lid to reveal *seledka pod shuboi*—a layered dish of sliced herring, cubed potatoes, and lots of other veggies. Farley grimaced. During the pack family gatherings, the Stravinskys usually brought some. My friends rarely ate it.

"Good to see both of you unharmed." Aunt Vera patted Will's arm. "What in heavens happened?"

Will opened his mouth, then quickly shut it again.

Aunt Vera leaned toward him like a vulture homing in a rumor-laden prey.

Mom plugged in her Crock-Pot. The rich smells of well-seasoned meat filled the kitchen. My empty stomach yanked me toward her.

"The insurance company is sorting things out," Thorn said. "But so far, the cabin is a total loss."

His words rang true, but it was what he hadn't revealed that made Aunt Vera nod slowly.

"That was such a beautiful house." Aunt Vera helped

herself to the food I left on my plate. "Your mama took such great care of it."

Now that I'd lost my spot, which I wouldn't mourn over, I fetched my aunt a warm cup of coffee. Two sugars and five creams, just the way she liked it.

After that, I stood next to my mother as she doled out servings onto plates. Why bother asking them if they wanted the roast or not? Food was food.

"How was your first day with the demons?" Mom examined me like a mama wolf checking her pup for knicks and cuts. "Your grandma was worried you'd find trouble." She knocked three times on the counter to ward evil away.

I recounted the peculiar shop that changed from day to night, but I didn't reveal the fairies or the strange spirits I'd encountered. Werewolves like my mother hated magic and all the dark intent connected with it. And for good reason. Long ago, she'd weathered an unfortunate incident with spellcasters.

"You're taking care of all those customers and not getting paid?" Mom asked.

Now that wasn't what I expected her to say next, but hey, I had bills to pay, too.

I told her how I had to repay my debt to Bill, who held me responsible for breaking into the rival thrift shop across the street from The Bends. "Stravinskys always repay their debts."

She shook her head and pursed her lips. "Those goblins are tricksters. Next thing you know, you'll owe the fairies at the bakery or the dwarves over at Dollar Tree for a shift or two. Keep your nose clean, Natalya."

I snatched the plate of roast. "I know. I've dug way too many holes. Time to patch up a few before I fall in."

Aunt Vera wiggled her fingers to beckon me to come to

her. "Come get some of Grandma's *seledka pod shuboi*. She worked her hands to the bone to make this for you."

I nodded and accepted two generous scoops, knowing very well Grandma had cooked the dish in an hour. Elaborating on my grandmother's misfortune was a tried-and-true Stravinsky guilt trip.

Will offered his seat to Mom, and they traded places. The youngest Grantham escaped out the back door before Farley could call after him.

"Wanna sit, Nat?" Thorn asked.

I shook my head and leaned against the counter to eat.

"Is she taking the day off, too?" Farley grumbled.

Thorn gave his dad the side-eye. Even the *clink-clink* from Aunt Vera as she stirred the creamfest in her cup stopped.

"She worked the night shift," Thorn said, "and spotted the fire on her way home from work." He glanced at me and jerked his chin toward the exit. *Go to sleep*, he mouthed.

I shook my head. Family had arrived and there was no way I'd leave them with Farley in such a foul mood.

"You and your boy will need clothes and things," Mom said gently. "I already called my church, and everyone is preparing care packages."

"I don't need their charity," Farley said stiffly.

"Charity?" Aunt Vera scoffed. "Your son will need clean clothes."

"He'll get them soon enough," Farley said. "The Granthams take care of their own."

Briefly, my gaze connected with Farley's, and I was the one to look away.

"How long do you plan to stay here?" Mom asked the question I wouldn't dare ask.

"Not for long." Farley slurped his juice and crumbs from his chin tumbled to the floor. "This home is too crowded."

"They have a spare bedroom, Farley." Aunt Vera tried to

lighten the mood. "Why don't you rest for a while and let your in-laws spoil you?"

He chuffed. "You might be able to ignore the trash in the living room, Vera, but I can't pretend it isn't there," he said matter-of-factly. "That type of behavior isn't normal."

The *seledka pod shuboi* in my mouth thickened.

Dr. Frank had told me once, "Anxiety disorders do have an effect on the family members of the sufferers. But with an open mind and dialogue, you can make progress toward resolving your issues with them."

Apparently, my father-in-law hadn't gotten the same chit-chat about an open mind.

Thorn stiffened, but Mom quickly spoke.

"Family is family," she said. "We don't get to choose what God gives us."

"No, we don't get a choice." Farley eyed me while he spoke. "But what I do know is that a pack should choose their members. Not a single man who chooses his *woman* over his pack."

Mom and Aunt Vera's heads swiveled to me at the same time.

"Go to sleep, Natalya," Aunt Vera said in Russian. The bite in her tone was unmistakable.

"But my food—" I said.

"*Eat later.*" My mother tilted her head in a way that used to frighten me as a child. Mama Wolf was about to throw down, and she didn't want me to see it.

The minute I left the room, I heard my mom say, "I've tolerated your behavior for years, Farley. But today if you want to fight with words, you should be ready to fight with your fists, too."

CHAPTER 4

Mom and Aunt Vera's raised voices carried through the hallways into the bedroom, where I jammed my earbuds into my ears. Soft musical numbers from Miles Davis would keep me occupied for hours. Thankfully, Miles had a discography to rival the ancient libraries in Alexandria. I sank into the blankets and practically rolled into the thick, dark blue comforter until I only had a hole to breathe out of.

Eventually, the house quieted down as my mom and aunt left, leaving father and son arguing in the kitchen. I paused the music. Thorn tried to keep his voice lowered, but I clearly heard my mate's warning.

"You're my father, and I'll always respect you, but this is my home," Thorn said firmly. "I won't let you belittle her without consequences."

Farley scoffed. "Why do you defend her? She's supposed to be an alpha now. You shouldn't have to protect her anymore."

"Should I let people like you walk all over her? Not

happening. Listen hard. You can't keep pushing people away. Mom wouldn't want you—"

"Don't bring her into this, boy." Farley's voice dropped to a menacing growl. "I don't want to hear it."

"You will keep hearing it," Thorn replied with as much vitriol. "I don't have to take your shit anymore. If you can't restrain yourself, you can stay somewhere else."

My muscles tensed up as I prepared to spring from the bed. If a fight broke out, Thorn would never forgive himself for striking his father.

More words were said, but I couldn't hear them. Over time, the house grew quiet again. At least their argument hadn't escalated further.

Somehow, I drifted off again. When I peeked at the nearby clock, it was barely past eight A.M. It felt like eons had gone by. An entire day could've passed.

Minutes ticked on by, and my eyelids drooped as the rise and fall of a jazz trumpet's mournful melody attempted to lull me into a good day's sleep. I could almost imagine Miles sitting on the stage, dressed in his jammies, beckoning me to slumber.

All that ended when thunderous gunfire and the heavy thuds of horses bled through the walls from the living room. Everything thumped the back of my head.

I rolled in my cocoon to face the opposite direction from the TV's noise, but the volume rose even higher.

God, or anybody who can reach that damn remote, please give me patience.

Between the raucous sound effects, I caught the harsh smacks of someone chewing potato chips. As hard as I tried not to imagine Farley sitting in his seat, like that day I'd approached him to rejoin the pack, I could only see him lounging away and letting chips fall into the La-Z-Boy's Mariana Trench-deep creases. And those bits would be beyond the reach of the longest attachment on my vacuum cleaner.

Well, there went sleeping. I lay there for a couple of minutes, wondering how to broach the subject of turning down the TV.

But I rode the guilt train along with my need for sleep. That man's house had burned down a couple of hours ago, and I wanted to march in there and take away the one thing Farley enjoyed.

I sighed. Thorn used to tell me how his parents watched those shows together when he was a kid. His mother often prepared supper, and they sat as a family and watched classics starring actors like John Wayne and Clint Eastwood. My family didn't watch those kinds of movies, but I could relate to the honeyed feeling that gathering with your family could bring. It was the memories of the past that helped us tolerate the present.

Resigned to my fate, I decided to get up. A glance at my phone revealed a text from Thorn: *I went to work. Hope you get some rest. Please understand all of this is temporary. Will is already looking for an apartment or a trailer.*

An apartment might be good for them. The place would be cool in the summer and warm in the winter, but werewolves like the Granthams preferred the woods. Even I lived this way. Farley wouldn't like anything Will found.

We needed another solution.

I took a shower and got dressed in my usual attire of a blouse and pencil skirt. When I prepared fresh coffee as a peace offering for Farley, I took my time. I even put the coffee on one of my favorite *Santa's Coming to Town* saucers. Triumphant I'd make a good impression, I plodded out to the living room to find Farley fast asleep.

Good God, the man had set the volume to movie-theater-ears-bleeding level and been asleep this whole time. I replaced his empty cup with the filled one, and then searched for the remote. Farley had a death grip around it.

Fine. He won the battle this time, but the war over controlling the TV had just begun. I could've used the buttons behind the TV to turn it off, but it was easier to leave it than fight him.

I considered returning to my room, but drowning out the noise would only annoy me further. Since it was still Tuesday morning, I could turn a downtrodden day around with a trip to New York City.

～

The drive into Manhattan relaxed the tension in my shoulders. Maybe it was the upcoming Christmas in July advertisements that bolstered my spirits. For a supernatural hiding among humans, small towns offered shops for our day-to-day needs, even a garage sale or two to find little gems, but the big metropolitan areas like New York City gave me a rush of anticipation. I could pretend to window-shop, slip through pawn shops without assessing eyes. Hell, the pawn shop owners welcomed shopping junkies like me with open paws.

Yes, come lose yourself in our thirty-percent-off sale, Natalya.

Indeed, I should.

As I found a spot for my car in a parking garage, I decided I'd settle my fix after I attended group therapy—my true reason for coming into the city. Shopping was a bonus round.

In quick time, I arrived at Dr. Frank's Upper East Side office. Right outside the meeting room, the receptionist greeted me and the sounds of my friends floated out. Once inside, everything was arranged as I expected. Eight seats formed a circle, with the large mahogany table moved to the wall. A lovely setting of fresh coffee and donuts sat on a small end table. Since I'd arrived right before the session started, I spotted four people milling around the seats. A chestnut-haired woman sat first. Abby the Muse's gaze was fixed out the tall windows along the wall, but she murmured to our friends once in a while. The poor woman had debilitating anxiety from her day job as a Muse to horror and thriller authors. Each day she witnessed their horrific plots and most twisted ideas to satisfy their readers. One recent assignment with a screenwriter in Los Angeles had left her withdrawn with dark eyes for days. But at least the script was going into rapid development at Netflix.

An Indian man wearing white gloves and a burnt-orange gamer T-shirt took a seat beside her. Raj was a minor Indian deity with as many cleanliness issues I had, but he was still an all-around cool guy. I hurried into the room and sat between two other therapy group members. I gave a halfhearted wave to a dwarf who looked nothing like the kind of creature you'd find in *The Lord of the Rings*. Tyler happened to look liked he just finished one of his modeling jobs. His blonde hair was messy but styled like you'd see in those glossy magazines. On my other side, I smiled at the only man in the room wearing all black.

"Good to see you, Nat," Nick said. "I thought you weren't coming this week due to your new job."

"It's a long story," I whispered.

"A long story you can tell everyone about," said an older man behind me.

Usually, Dr. Frank materialized into one of the seats, but today he walked in human-style. If I could teleport everywhere in a flashy mist or bright supernova style, I'd do it all the time.

"You don't want to hear this one," I replied.

"He does," Nick said flatly.

"Good morning, everyone!" Dr. Frank said in his usual warm tone. He glanced around the circle, and I waited for him to do his usual hocus-pocus to reduce the anxiety in the room.

Instead, he checked his watch.

"Is something wrong?" Tyler asked, broaching the very subject I wanted to know.

Bring on the good stuff, Doc.

"She's almost here." Dr. Frank peeked at his watch again before he turned to the door.

A woman wearing a plaid sundress two sizes too big waltzed through the door pushing a black-and-white stroller. A heavy fog of perfume with hints of nightshade and lavender accompanied her.

"Thanks for waiting for me, Dr. Frank." Lilith the soul-eating succubus joined us. When she noticed Nick had no free spots next to him, she took a spot next to Abby.

"Not a problem. I see you brought your daughter this time instead of using her as an excuse not to attend," Dr. Frank said jokingly, and that got a dry laugh from the succubus.

The Muse's face brightened. "Is that your new baby?"

"That's my Aleksandra." Lilith beamed at the stroller. "Just like her mama, she likes to prowl at night."

I cringed. I wouldn't associate prowling with an infant, but the dark-haired baby appeared content, wrapped in blankets as she snoozed with a light snore. She reminded me of my beautiful nine-month-old niece, Sveta.

"Now that everyone is here, we can begin." Dr. Frank's magic slipped through the room. Every worry I'd hauled with me to New York fell to the floor. My toes curled, and the heavenly sigh from Raj reflected my very thoughts: Dr. Frank might have us addicted to this stuff.

"Now that we've reduced our anxiety levels, let's recap

from last week. During that session, we talked about using our cognitive behavior therapy, which is our Swiss army knife of exercises, to combat behaviors that induce anxiety. Does anyone have any thoughts on your assignments from last week?"

Tyler spoke first. "I spoke to a matchmaker over the phone last weekend." He let out a long breath. "Some of the clans in Southern California would like for me to go to Los Angeles the next time I'm booked for a gig there."

"That's great to hear." Dr. Frank eyed him. "You don't sound excited, though."

"I'm absolutely terrified," Tyler admitted. "I've been rejected too many times. I wonder why I bother to try to make myself acceptable to other dwarves."

A knowing hush fell over the room. Rejection reigned.

Dr. Frank looked around to make sure he had our attention. "I'd like to go deeper with that word: acceptable. What do you define as acceptable?"

No one spoke for a bit.

"The definition is different for everyone," I finally said, "but to me, acceptable is hiding what others perceive as flawed. We're all putting on a mask of normalcy."

"We're supernatural creatures," Dr. Frank said. "We're already hidden. We shouldn't have to hide ourselves from those with whom we share a common purpose."

"No, we shouldn't," I said as frustration made my back straighten. "But it's unfair how the mistakes from our past, mistakes related to our mental illnesses, keep coming back. That no matter how hard we work to better ourselves, there's always another hill up the road to climb."

I told them about my father-in-law's home burning down and how he lived with me now. After I gave them the very short yet painful version of our history together, I wasn't as sad. Revealing my past felt like pulling thorns from my paws, but Dr. Frank nodded to offer encouragement.

"Telling ourselves we need to persevere isn't enough sometimes." We all turned to Nick. "After I returned home from medical school—as a failure—I kept telling myself I had to keep trying. I had to go back. I had to get over my own weaknesses, but most days, I feel like it's easier to give up than keep trying."

Nodding heads circled the room.

Lilith took that moment to add her wisdom. "I feel the same way. I'm a single parent now." She touched the stroller. "I have to be her mother and father now."

"Did something happen to Yuri?" I asked.

Lilith had married my cousin Yuri from Saint Petersburg, Russia. A year ago, the two chatted it up over the phone, and once my lazy cousin fell for the succubus, she headed to Russia and they got married. Even worse, Yuri never had many aspirations or goals. He lived as a band performer, but I thought the pair would stay together and settle down.

"He disappeared. That's what happened." Her lower lip trembled. "He ran away like everyone else."

Damn, that's messed up. Tonight, I'd have to make a little phone call to his mom. Having the Stravinsky clan in Russia hunt you down the old-school way meant an ass beating was coming. His punishment wouldn't be pretty.

"Now that you're back in New York, do you have a plan to get yourself back on your feet?" Dr. Frank offered a reassuring smile. "You have a child to support, and one thing I know about you is that you're driven and confident. Those are the qualities your little girl needs right now."

Lilith appeared thoughtful for the first time—ever. Usually, she opened her mouth and said the first thing that came to mind. The room grew quiet until she spoke. Maybe motherhood had changed the succubus.

"I want to be a good mom, first of all, and that means getting my strength back," she admitted. "I just need to find a way to feed on the souls of my victims and tackle the babysitting thing."

Nope, she hadn't learned a damn thing. Once a sex demon, always a sex demon.

Dr. Frank turned to the others, effectively diverting that wayward football pass. "Raj, you never told us about what happened during your therapy exercise at your job."

Raj sat up straighter. "Abby was kind enough to offer support during a job-related exercise at the game development company where I work."

Abby piped up. "Raj's workplace is really nice. I wish I got assignments there."

"How did it go?" Nick asked.

"As well as it could," Raj said. "I had a meeting with the game developers…"

"And they don't shower often," Abby added.

I shuddered, understanding how Raj wanted to be a part of the team, yet not lose his damn mind over his coworkers' cleanliness habits. My friend went into detail how he survived the meeting without reminding everyone about the free showers in the building or the supply of soap he gave as holiday presents last year. (A rather clever idea, if I may say so.)

After Raj finished, Dr. Frank gave us our assignments for next week. Abby had to attend a workshop or two at the upcoming Thriller Writers Festival in town, while Tyler had to attend a dwarf activity with confidence.

Dr. Frank paused to smile at each of us. "There's so much potential in this group." His eyes softened. "I'm looking forward to the day when you won't need an old man like me, but for now, let's get to work."

When Dr. Frank faced me, my stomach sank. I never liked

his idea of work. That white wizard knew how to rub my fur the wrong way. "Natalya, I want you to remember that every setback is a test against your resolve to get better. I believe you shouldn't skip therapy, even with your night job this week. I want you to craft or buy a gift for your father-in-law with Nick's help. Your father-in-law must accept this gift with an open heart."

My mouth dropped open. Right now, I couldn't think of anything I wanted to give that bitter wolf.

Dr. Frank continued. "Nick is facing a setback too. After he returned from medical school, I advised him to volunteer at a local free clinic for warlocks, but he hasn't."

Nick sighed. He had healed me plenty of times. What would stop him from healing anybody now?

"You two have similar conditions, and when presented with exercises, you don't let the other divert from the proper path." Our therapist nodded sagely, but I crossed my arms. As much as I wanted to help Nick, the very idea of giving a gift to the man who referred to me as inferior left a foul taste in my mouth. All Farley really deserved was a hairball coughed up on his feet.

CHAPTER 5

After therapy ended, I wanted to chat with Nick, but he vanished in a spectacular flash of white light. Rather clever of him. He wouldn't be able to elude me for long, though, 'cause thanks to Dr. Frank, I knew where that sly white wizard lived.

I tried to stroll through Brooklyn and even browse a few shops, but Dr. Frank's exercise weighed heavily on my mind. If I was petty, I could've grabbed the cheapest tourist bauble in one of the stores here, but my therapist's additional constraint corralled me: Thorn's father had to accept it with an open heart.

I snorted. Open heart? Did that grumpy wolf still *have* one?

A year ago, I thought Farley had that contagious disease going around—being a raging asshole. My parents taught me to respect my elders, but over the past year I'd learned a new lesson: I shouldn't take people's shit anymore.

This particular antique shop had a lovely display with antique German music boxes sat off to the side. On any other day, I would've admired the tinkling sound of the *Für Elise* melody, but today I left without an afterthought.

Right now, the only thing Farley needed from me was a warm place to sleep and a hearty "have a nice day" when I helped him move into another place.

My machismo lasted most of the drive home, but by the time pulled up to the cottage, I changed into a sniveling pup.

I didn't want to go home.

And I had to work in a couple of hours and needed a place to go.

As I passed The Bends, I longed to go inside. Maybe I could pass off a couple of hours at my old job and pretend everything was better. I sighed and dismissed that idea. Bill expected me to complete my assignment with the demons before I returned to my usual haunt. So I went to the one place no one would judge me: Barney's. Aggie worked as a manager during the day shift. Maybe she'd take pity and let me hide there. Thorn wouldn't take that well, but what about bonding with my bestie?

Barney's restaurant was nestled not far off the outskirts of town. Most folks said it was in Toms River city proper, but we claimed it, so the townsfolk had another establishment to eat at other than Archie's Burgers, McDonald's, and the questionable chicken joint right off the Parkway.

I strolled into the restaurant, hoping for a cup of coffee and a booth where I could stare into space for the next couple of hours. The last time I visited a week or so ago, I'd worried about the Basilisk King and the little chests he'd left all over the damn place. It was refreshing to come inside like a regular old customer. My usual table in the far back was free.

The owner was some gal who'd bought the establishment from the man who built the place. She'd remodeled the place back when I was a kid, replacing the seventies-style bright orange booths with modern blue-painted tables and black chairs with navy-blue fabric seats. The Coney Island decor was based, or so the rumor said, on the owner's childhood in Long Island. Normally, due to their poorly wiped surfaces, I didn't bother eating here, but now that Aggie had taken over as manager again, the tile floors gleamed from a recent polish, and I couldn't miss the lemony fresh scent of bacteria-killing chemicals.

I headed up to the counter to order a soda and a bag of chips. Might as well have something to eat instead of coffee. After two helpings of Grandma's *seledka pod shuboi*, I'd be good until I started work. Grandma added enough mayonnaise for days.

I was surprised to see a familiar face greet me. "Welcome to Barney's, Natalya."

"Long time no see, Brenna. I gotta be honest, I didn't expect to see you here."

The earth witch laughed, giving me a glimpse of the playful dimple in her right cheek. "My parents are surprised, too. I'm supposed to be living it up in Europe with my cushy teaching job at a medical school."

After she admitted she should be teaching at some prestigious institution overseas, instead of punching buttons at a part-time gig, I felt a bit weird. Back when I'd first met her, not too long ago, she came off as mellow and pretty cool. If I hadn't known what spells she could cast, I would've thought she was a Martha's Vineyard socialite with chin-length dark hair and a willowy frame.

And yet she was still here. Was she still seeing Nick? I hoped so. Nick deserved to find someone who would love him for his true self.

Aggie appeared from the kitchen as Brenna finished ringing up my order.

"Hey, Nat. Whatcha doin' here?" Seeing my best friend at

her place of work always threw me off. Aggie rocked casual clothes all the time, but when she put on her managerial khaki pants and polo shirt, she transformed her Clark Kent style.

"You heard the Grantham place burned down?" I asked.

"Yeah, are they okay?" Aggie asked.

Even Brenna appeared concerned.

"They're fine," I said with a sigh, "but Farley's set up camp at my place."

"Ouch." Aggie grimaced.

I gestured to the witch. "You weren't kidding when you said you wanted to hire her, Aggie."

"She's horribly overqualified," Aggie said with a snort.

"And underpaid," Brenna added, her faint Southern accent coming through.

"Yes, that," Aggie admitted, "but Brenna told me she's the new Witches' Guild rep for the area."

I turned to Brenna, who winked at me. Now that was some news.

"After She Who Always Walks the Path veered close to the county, the guild wanted a presence from the sisterhood to watch out for trouble."

"You mean watch over the South Toms River Pack," I grumbled.

Brenna gave an apologetic smile. "That too."

I picked up the tray with my order. "I guess I'd rather it be you than someone else with ill intent. Most spellcasters don't have the pack's best interests in mind."

As I sat at the far table and munched on my chips, I considered the spellcasters. Every now and then, Thorn remarked that he'd spotted a warlock here or there, but they'd never interfered with pack business. That was still too close for my comfort. I looked forward to the day when everything quieted down in this town.

After killing my bag of chips and draining two servings of Coke, I played sudoku on my phone and checked my email five times. I even called Grandma to thank her for the food and made a call to Russia to give my aunt an earful about my cousin Yuri. After that, boredom snuck into Barney's and sank its vicious teeth into my hide.

With the lunch crowd gone, afternoon eaters came and went. Which left me an opportunity to offer a hand or two.

"Stop feeling up the ketchup, Nat." Aggie snuck up on me while I did the deed.

She caught me lining up the condiments on the tables. A big party had left, and I wanted to tidy up the tables. "I'm *free* help."

Aggie frowned at the three bottles and separated them at uneven intervals.

"That's pure evil," I murmured.

"Don't you need to go to work soon? Maybe go home?"

Home flashed before my eyes, but it didn't feel that way.

"Fine." As I gathered my things, I gave her the evil eye and plotted how I'd thwart her attempts next time.

With nowhere to go, I gave up and made my way toward the river to start my shift early. Might as well see if I could get some bonus hours in to pay off my debt sooner.

I pulled into the parking lot to find plenty of customers browsing the wares outside. I immediately spotted the short woman I'd met yesterday. This time, she wore an even brighter smile along with a mauve "Cats Are My Kids" T-shirt and enough multicolored clips in her dark brown hair to open a hair-clip mart.

"Good afternoon, Natalya!" She tucked her hands into her capri pants pockets. "You're here rather early."

After she answered questions from a customer about purchasing a kiln setup, I followed her into the cool confines of the store. We stopped briefly at the cash register so I could don one of the maroon aprons.

"When my sister told me she hired someone," she said softly, "I was worried she'd brought on someone lazy, but you seem all right."

"Thanks for the compliment." I held back a chuckle. "My family taught me early that whether I work for a week or a single day, giving half the effort is as the same as giving no effort at all."

"Wise words, indeed."

I stared harder at the day demon, waiting to glimpse the layers of magic covering her, but Dayla appeared—hell, she *smelled*—like an average human. Even her toothy smile exuded sunshine.

But even I wasn't foolish enough to trust a demon.

"May I ask a question?" Might as well get some answers, since Dayla came off as less prickly than Mimi.

"Sure thing." She paused before checking the tag on a beautiful stone wolf with a butterfly perched on its nose.

"Mimi seems like she has everything under control on the Midnight Barge. She could even move that cloaked lady in the day store over to the barge to work the register. Why did she want more help?"

That got an exasperated sigh. "She's always wanted more. More profits. More extravagant customers. A customer a day would suit me just fine."

"Sounds like you're the kind of girl that likes the simple life."

"Pretty much. We had a better life back in Canada. I had a

gorgeous tree farm with Japanese maples and Christmas trees."

I grinned. Nothing beat fresh fir and spruce trees for the holidays.

Dayla continued with an annoyed expression. "We made a tidy profit until She Who Always Walks the Path veered away. After that, we earned less money, and she dragged me to this town."

"Why didn't you stay behind?" It sounded like Dayla had made a home for herself. Why give it up?

"Because no matter how much your family drives you crazy, they're still family. My sister and I are two sides of a coin that will never agree to anything, but we can never be apart."

As someone with a sibling, I could relate. Time to earn my keep. "Where would you like me to start?"

"Not sure. Pretty soon, the day shift will end. Why don't you go down the aisles and tidy up?"

When I hurried to get to work, I caught her amused giggle.

Did I appear a little too eager to clean?

With a bounce in my step, I began my task, pausing here and there to direct customers. Next, I found my nirvana. My place of bliss. I arranged the wares back into perfect lines.

Right around eight in the evening, as the sun touched the horizon, I kept working and waited for the customers to do their strange shuffle to the exits. But the couple next to me continued to debate the placement in their home of an absolutely hideous set of ceramic plates the color of blended bird shit. An elderly man examining sake drinking cups kept picking up and putting down the same cup.

I glanced outside. The sky deepened to rosy pinks, a shiver coursed over me, and the wolf within me whined. Something wasn't right. I couldn't spot Dayla outside or in the store. A quick check at the rear of the mart revealed the back office doors had switched places.

This store made as much sense as the ingredient labels on the cheap processed food from the Dollar Mart.

Cautiously, I approached the back door, taking my time to turn the doorknob and venture outside. Instead of seeing twilight and a sky blossoming with starlight and choppy clouds, I saw the sun slowly descending as if the star clawed its way to the horizon. The air was far more humid, thick with dampness that weighed heavily in my chest with each breath. An ominous fog gathered on the riverbank. I couldn't make out whether the Midnight Barge had arrived until my feet touched the hard surface of what had to be the pier's rough planks.

A powerful urge to go back the way I came flicked at me. Wasn't I here to do my job and not get myself killed? And yet curiosity, and the drive to perform my duties on the barge, propelled me forward until I reached the plank. Once I boarded the ship, I waited for the night demon to appear, but she remained elusive while I scanned the Main Deck's interior. Everything appeared in its place until I came to the third room. An empty spot in a display caught my eye, and my stomach dropped.

Had someone purchased the whistle during the daytime?

No, I'd stood here until the final night customer departed, and no one had bought the mysterious dog whistle. I searched through the room. Maybe a new creature I hadn't met before had cleaned up the shop and misplaced it.

But not a single fingerprint or a trace of a scent marked the passage of a cleaner or a thief.

So what in the hairy hell happened?

I hurried out to the Main Deck to find my employer standing next to the railing.

"We have a problem. The whistle's—"

I paused at the sight of Mademoiselle Midnight's ashen face as she pointed to the riverbank. The fog appeared to part at her command.

Nestled among the tall grass, cattails, and wild geraniums lay the prone figure of a dead body.

CHAPTER 6

My heart jumped up to my throat, did a double somersault, then bounded into the water. I didn't speak. I raced down the plank and along the muddy riverbank, flicking away cattails and river brush to amble my way to the fallen form.

As I got closer though, I slowed down.

This didn't seem like a regular body. As I crept toward the figure, I expected to find telltale signs someone had passed. Death had a smell you never forgot. And yet something far deeper seeped into my nostrils and coursed along my tongue: the heady, woodsy scent of the high full moon when I walked as a wolf and the full bloom of nightshade on the darkest nights. All these things pulsed through me.

I peered at the poor creature that lay on its back. It wore nothing more than a simple black T-shirt and a pair of jeans. The body appeared to be a male humanoid, but its skin had turned a sickly shade of gray that grew darker with each second. Was it a man or a woman? The glint from a river pebble's shine caught my eyes. The smooth rock was strung on the vine from a moonflower plant and wrapped around the creature's ankle. Even the short strands of its hair resembled moonflower vines.

How peculiar.

I reached forward with a shudder. I mean, damn, maybe I should try to perform CPR. As much my entire being cringed at the idea of putting my mouth on someone else's and breathing life into them, doing the right thing far outweighed my own fears.

I pressed my hand against its back. Could I be mistaken, and it lived?

"It's dead," Mademoiselle Midnight said behind me.

My heart stumbled at her unexpected arrival, but I remained steady.

"Was this one of our customers?" I managed to ask with cotton in my mouth. I had yet to have a customer knock off in my store.

"No, it was my night guard," she said somberly. "It patrols the ship during the daytime until the barge opens."

"Damn." I backed up, careful to look around me for any evidence from the fight that occurred. "Is the thief still here?" I whispered.

"I don't know. During the daytime, I sleep deeply."

Other than the gurgles of frogs and the buzzing from bothersome mosquitos, nothing stirred along the Toms River.

Mud leaked into my clean shoes, but I ignored the unpleasant, yet cool sensation. Safety first. Panic button later.

I glanced down at the body. If someone had stolen the whistle, they also knew how to take out the night guard. I had to understand what the night guard could do before I considered the worst. "What kind of creature is this?"

"It's made from night things."

"Night things?"

"I gathered shadows formed from the moonlight, intertwined the moon's reflection on the water, and gave it breath from nightshade." She folded her arms as if everyone did that kind of thing.

I gave a nod. Calling the police wasn't an option at this point. The creature wasn't a human, thank goodness, but a problem remained. During the daytime, something had broken into the Midnight Barge, plowed through the poor night guard, then stolen the dog whistle.

"Could that fairy have done this?" I asked.

"Maybe. Her powers aren't strong enough to take out a night guard during the half-moon, but if she had help, she could."

The fairy had a good enough motive to do this, but as I scanned the riverbank for signs of the intruder's escape path, I only found a set of large footprints. These appeared far larger than a human's, and the fairy I'd seen the other day wore Louboutins no larger than the span of my hand.

No new scents other than the overwhelming river muck, either.

The clouds parted, and more shadows receded. I could see more evidence of the fight, but it was the growing frown on Mademoiselle Midnight's face that caught my attention. Around the body, I spied spots where the cattails appeared split open. What had caused that?

It wasn't the cattails that set off alarm bells, but another set of prints in the mud, buried between the river plants. It was a set of paw prints large enough to be a werewolf's.

CHAPTER 7

Two more night guards arrived from the barge to do the night demon's bidding. They had a similar appearance as the first creature, but they stared at us with vacant expressions and black stones for eyes. My chest grew tighter and tighter as one guard removed the body while the other waited. I wished I knew what had happened.

"Secure the boat," she said to the other one.

As I watched the night guard return to the boat, I wondered if this place wasn't safe anymore. Not once in my time with Bill had anyone broken into The Bends. Of course, after watching Bill's thrift store defend itself during the attack from the basilisks, I had a better idea what tricks and such the goblin kept from me.

Unfortunately, the Midnight Barge didn't employ such measures.

I hungered to track the larger footprints and the pawprints to see where they led.

"What would you like for me to do?" I asked her. "Do we need to close the store for the night?"

"The store will open, Nadia." She stared silver-tipped daggers at the pawprints I'd seen. "But *you* won't be working here tonight. You and *your* people have already caused enough trouble."

"My people?" I shuffled back from her. "You believe my pack would do this?"

"That's a werewolf print." She scoffed and the deep purples in her peplum top deepened. "Have you seen any coyotes or wolves shopping for *deals* along the river? You probably told one of your friends to come take it, didn't you? With one blow, you can call Cerberus and the hellhound could drive Diana and her hunting dogs elsewhere."

Her short height stretched upward until her black eyes met mine. Thunderclouds snapped and hissed in her irises as her tiny mouth opened to reveal teeth like jagged shards of glass. Her fingers flexed, revealing the brightened and smoldering tips of her fingers.

"If I believed you'd be capable of stealing the whistle, I would've ripped you in two," she snapped. "But someone else did it. You're going to find out who it was."

I stumbled backward. A growl formed in my chest, but I stopped myself.

I had no idea what havoc real-life demons could unleash, and my internal organs didn't want a demonstration. I'd seen *The Exorcist*, thank you very much. While a head-spinning demon might not faze me, one vomiting pea soup sure as hell would.

"Fourteen days. That's all the time I'll give you." She began to walk away but paused. "Nora, don't bother showing up tomorrow evening or the day after unless you have the whistle or evidence of the true culprit."

She took another two steps away from me before the fog along the riverbank swept through and sucked her away.

At this point, I knew she deliberately used the wrong name to fuck with me. And I didn't like it.

Instead of sitting around like a damn fool and wondering what to do next, I did what any werewolf with OCD would do: I made a beeline to my car to compose myself. But no amount of wet wipes or deep breaths would calm my racing heart. As hard as I tried to scrap away the mud and my encounter with Mademoiselle Midnight, I couldn't stop thinking about her sharp teeth or her smoke-tinged claws waiting to strike.

She'd nipped me for a reason. It was a warning. All werewolves established a hierarchy that way: give a bite to the wolves you need to keep in line, and in doing so, her true self gave me a glimmer of her infernal powers. I damn well knew she could've struck me dead. Instead, now I had a deal with a devil.

I shuddered to imagine what the rest of her looked like.

Twenty minutes later, the crickets continued to chirp and lure their lady friends out to play while I gathered my senses. When I could stand without shivering, I slipped out of my car and unlocked the trunk. Tucked inside a hidden compartment along the side was my goblin blade. This handy weapon ended up in my possession while I was helping my dad with his moon debt a year ago. While questioning a goblin mechanic, he tried to attack me with the little silver blade, and I took it from him. Unbeknownst to me, the goblin blade transformed into a new weapon based on the nearest supernatural threat to the owner's proximity. As hard as I tried to find the goblin mechanic's shop, the fellow had disappeared. Which meant I had to use it wisely until I could return it to the original owner.

With the goblin blade tucked into a sheath strapped to my belt, I left the ornamental stone mart parking lot to track the footprints and pawprints. Without a scent, I'd have trouble following the culprit, but persistence was a motivator like no other. When I returned to the riverbank, I easily spotted the scorch marks and footprints remained. I circled around them a couple of times, checking the bushes and plants for any trace evidence like hair or bits of clothing. I uncovered none, so I'd have to work with the prints for now.

As luck would have it, the trail didn't lead into the water, but headed south, away from the ceramic mart. I darted southward along the backside of a small bait shop, a tanning salon, and a pizzeria. The enticing scent of pizzas and wings tugged me toward the restaurant, but I ignored it to continue my search.

Soon enough, the patches of grass behind the business complex ended and I encountered concrete. Any lazy wolf would've given up, but I suspected whoever did this would avoid cameras and humans. I stuck behind the businesses and, after doubling back seven times, hit pay dirt when I crossed Atlantic City Boulevard and headed west to the houses along Lakeview Drive. The expansive backyards left plenty of hiding places, but the goblin blade remained quiet and inert in the sheath. If a threat loomed near, I'd have to get closer.

As I followed the prints southwest from yard to yard, I considered the potential culprit. Those prints came from a large wolf of some kind. Could another werewolf in the area, who knew about the Midnight Barge, have killed the night guard, and then stolen the whistle for themselves? The faces of my friends and family came to mind, but none of them had mentioned knowing about the mystical goods at the ceramic mart. If Mademoiselle Midnight and the Daylight Dame had recently relocated here to cash in on the new fairy path, then the thief would know about them, too.

And in small towns, news travelled quickly.

This whole situation felt like a growing pile of dog shit in the middle of the road. Anyone could step into it and stroll into *my* yard.

I ventured farther south, the only lights illuminating my passage were the moon and the occasional streetlights. This early in the evening, I caught the familiar sounds of families griping about bills and the scrapes of knife and forks hitting plates.

Wait, did I smell well-seasoned smothered pork chops?

I ignored the distractions and watched out for danger. Here and there, I even could discern the large footprints, as well as the wolf walking with them. Like any animal, it veered away from its companion to sniff interesting things like nearby fences or posts. But the animal never stopped long enough to leave traces of itself. Very interesting. 'Cause Uncle Boris would've peed on a post or two to mark his territory.

"Can't have some rogue thinkin' we're weak," he'd boast.

Houses grew fewer and farther between as I navigated through the southern edge of town. When I arrived at the intersection of Double Trouble Road and Brookforest Drive, only one destination remained: Jake Branch County Park.

The park didn't have the breadth and depth of nearby Double Trouble State Park, but with over four hundred acres, the perpetrators I was tracking had plenty of cover if they decided to go deeper into Double Trouble State Park to the immediate south.

When I picked up my pace, the wolf within me sang and howled as I parted the brush to enter her home. Wilderness areas brought out my most primal instincts. My need to hunt was sated, since I'd run during the full moon a couple days ago, but my drive to find the culprit grew tenfold.

After tracking the prints for a while, I came to a clearing and scanned the ground for the next set of prints. One set veered left into the tall summer grass, while the other set went to the right. Damn it. Of course they'd gone in separate directions.

A barred owl roosting in a tree hooted above me as I paused to inhale and separate the scents. I found nothing but foraging animals like whitetail deer and summer fowl. They'd crossed this field recently. While they were fun to chase, they weren't what I was after.

Yet a tingle on the back of my neck made me freeze. I backed up a bit and listened. Branches broke in the distance on the other side of the field to my left. Bushes rustled in the distance, imperceptible to human ears. No small rabbits made that sound.

A larger predator loomed nearby.

The goblin blade twitched in the sheath. I stooped and wished I had the downwind advantage. If one of these creatures was a werewolf, it'd know I tracked it here. Not good.

Packs often used a divide-and-conquer strategy to take down prey, and I wasn't interested in being anybody's dinner.

I retrieved the goblin blade, expecting to see a silver glint in the moonlight, but the weapon changed from silver to muted orange. The knife handle curved in my palm into a C shape as the blade stretched out from the new handle into a shield the size of my torso. Flaming spikes formed on the surface. Damn, this was different. The fire illuminated the field around me. In the past, the goblin blade always formed an offensive weapon. Maces. Swords. Spears.

But what did a *shield* mean?

I advanced deeper into the field. If someone attacked me from the tree line, I'd never see them coming. Sweat formed on my palms and my grip grew slippery. I wiped off one hand on my skirt, then the other. I'd almost reached the center. The clearing fell silent except for the thunderous beats of my heart. Nothing good happened when all went quiet. *Shit.*

Time to call for the cavalry. In the past, I'd had an argument or two with my mate about fighting alone. He had a good point there, so I fished out my phone with one hand and sent an SOS text with my location attached.

See? I could learn from my *many* mistakes.

Thorn immediately tried to return the call, filling the field with my phone's shrill ringtone. I might as well have sent up a flare to every supernatural predator within hearing distance. With a curse, I silenced the phone.

I could sense something coming, but I couldn't make out any shadows along the tall grass. The pervasive hush smothered the field. I held my breath and braced myself behind the shield. Suddenly, from my far left, a large form rose from the grass, then a heavy weapon struck the shield with a bone-rattling clang. The force took my breath away as the strike reverberated up my arms. I jerked forward to use the spikes to parry, but I hit nothing. Another foe came up fast behind me and rammed my side. As I careened through the air, the raw pain, like a burning wound from a basilisk's claw, spread along my torso. Shield in hand, I landed in the trees, smacking, slamming, and knocking into the sharp branches as gravity brought me down. One limb even slapped me in the face, leaving the harsh tang of blood in my mouth.

Though it wasn't the trees that took me out, but the perfectly placed rock right below.

Sweet nightmares, Natalya.

CHAPTER 8

When I came to, I had no idea how much time had passed, only that I was in horrible pain and the light through the curtains in my bedroom were far too bright.

My eyelids drooped shut as pain swooped in to draw me back to sleep, but I forced my heavy eyelids open to focus on the present. If I wanted answers as to what happened, I had to return to the here and now—even if I didn't want a reminder of how much I hurt. I shifted, and sharp pain down my side made me suck in a breath.

Now, I'd had my ass kicked a couple times. I'd even had a near-death experience that left me licking my wounds and cursing my incessant desire to protect my pack. Smart folks walked away. They called for backup. I'd done one out of two, but the enemy I had yet to identify still snuck up on me and got me good.

I held still and looked around. I lay in my bedroom in the cottage. Plenty of blankets covered me, and the ceiling fan circulated cool air through the room. The ear-splitting sounds of Yul Brynner and Steven McQueen riding to victory in *The Magnificent Seven* bled through the wall. Yet another western. No rest for the weary, eh?

A hand touched my face. I turned my head to see Thorn.

"I'd ask what happened," I murmured, my voice dry and thick, "but I have a feeling you didn't find anything."

He sighed and carefully drew me close until my head rested on his shoulder. "What were you doing out there?"

"Long story."

He gave me a drink of water. "I'm not going anywhere. Let's try this again. What happened to you?"

I told him the whole story. How the spring fairy showed up for the whistle, then up to the next day when I discovered the missing whistle and the dead night guard. Finally, I revealed the night demon's dire warning to recover the whistle before some idiot blew it and unleashed a three-headed hellhound.

When I finished, Thorn didn't speak. During his tenure so far as alpha over the pack, we'd had to fight for our lives a couple of times. It was in our best interest not to jump in snout first.

He offered me another sip and finally said, "Trouble always has a way of finding us."

"It's imperative we find the thief...but where do we even start?"

"How do we know if someone hasn't blown the whistle already?" he asked slowly.

Good question. "Have there been any three-headed dog sightings?"

"Are you serious?" He frowned.

"I'm sure we wouldn't miss a hellhound stampede, but I'm not sure if one of the pack members would use the whistle to drive She Who Always Walks the Path away." I had no immediate plans to check the Sourland Mountain Preserve to see if the goddess lingered nearby. My last trip to the reserve had left me in her clutches. I wouldn't have made it home if it wasn't for Mevelyn. She'd sacrificed herself for me, and now I had a debt I might never be able to repay.

An itch on the back of my head made my eyes twitch, but I ignored it. Pain along my side lit up like five-million-volt Christmas lights.

"And how dangerous is Mademoiselle Midnight?" Thorn asked.

I recalled the night demon's show of strength. "She's dangerous. I wouldn't want to face her without a couple of wizards."

Thorn's jaw jerked. "I don't want you working there anymore."

"You don't have to tell me twice. She doesn't want me back anyway."

We sat together for a while, listening to the movie. Then he leaned down and kissed my forehead gently. The tension in his shoulders hadn't eased. My news hadn't gone over well.

"The pack needs to gather and figure out what to do," he said. "We'll form search parties. Maybe whatever attacked you is still in the area."

I tried to get up, but he pressed my shoulder down. "I'll call the pack healer to check on you. Rest now."

After Thorn left to make some phone calls, I tried to rest, but with a shootout every couple of minutes, all I could do was stare wide-eyed at the ceiling. Maybe I could meditate or something.

Twenty minutes later, our pack healer arrived to assess my injuries. The lovely woman in her mid-fifties smelled like the coffee candy I used to get from Grandma. During her not-so-gentle examination, I learned I had third-degree burns.

"What hit you?" she asked once she wrapped up the exam.

"No idea, but if it burned me, I don't understand why my clothes didn't catch on fire."

"You didn't see any flames?"

"Other than the open flames on my shield, no."

She hummed. "Maybe the creature excretes a corrosive substance like the basilisks, except through its skin. The good news is your body is healing well. You're not showing any signs of infection like after a basilisk bite. We just need to keep removing the dead skin as it sloughs off."

Did she say *slough* off?

The healer was cheerful and all, but I couldn't stop thinking about gooey dead skin. And thank goodness I had a diagnosis this time. Those basilisk cuts I got not too long ago had nearly killed me. Thanks to my friend Nick, I'd survived. Speaking of that white wizard, I should figure out how to do our exercise once I didn't feel like shit anymore.

Usually, Nick hounded me to do our therapy activities together, but this time he had yet to knock on my door or send me a text. That was a sure sign he didn't want to face this particular exercise any more than I did.

I sighed and tried to rest. My body needed time to do its job. The pack would meet tonight, and if I had to hobble in there to warn everyone, I'd do it and then sleep off the pain later.

Somehow, I dozed off until the stampede of what had to be a thousand horses jolted me awake. The warm hues of the sun setting outside the window told me I'd slept for at least eight hours, but even that much time had only dulled the pain a little. I still gingerly got up. The dressings provided little protection. Each step from my bed to the bathroom had me mewling like a pup. When I made it to the middle of the hallway, the TV went silent.

Oh God, am I that loud?

I waited to hear Farley's complaints. Maybe he'd tell me

these wounds might toughen up a weakling like me. I got nothing and safely shuffled into the bathroom. I shut the door behind me and considered how I'd manage a shower and, even worse, figure out how to squat and do my business without stretching the skin along my side.

For the first time in my life, I wished I could do the deed standing up.

Hopefully, for the last time.

By the time I left the bathroom, squeaky clean and slightly pissed from how many times I'd moved the wrong way, the TV blared as usual. Thank goodness I didn't have to go through the living room to get to the kitchen. I was in no shape to witness the crumbs, chips, and other snacks Farley had dropped on the floor.

The shit will still be there tomorrow, I promised myself.

Once in the kitchen, I searched the freezer to find most of the TV dinners gone. Only one remained: a long-forgotten freezer-burned dinner tucked in the back with blocks of frozen meat. Might as well see what I'd find after I chipped away the icicles. After I crammed the cardboard container's contents into the microwave, I watched the glass tray spin inside. I considered calling my mom to bring me some food, but I sucked it up and let the meal cook.

Once the microwave gave a triumphant beep, I snagged the food and stared at a sad plastic tray with a mound of mashed potatoes, a withered chocolate brownie, and a soggy piece of fried chicken. I almost laughed. (Glad I didn't. That would've hurt.) I still ate the food—like a stiff robot, mind you, but I managed to finish my meal.

By the time Thorn came home from work to check on me before the meeting, I was ready to go.

"No, you're not ready to go." Thorn gave me an exasperated expression, but I'd already slipped on a pair of flats. My usual uniform of a pencil skirt and blouse were replaced with an oversized *Santa Stole My Cheer* T-shirt and sweatpants that I'd barely fastened.

"Shouldn't you rest right now?" he said softly. "You're still breathing heavily."

Why hadn't his father asked me that earlier?

"I'll be fine." I cracked a smile. Might've been a grimace, but Thorn had seen both before.

Thorn took one more look at me, shook his head, then headed out to the SUV.

Ten minutes later, we pulled into the parking lot next to Archie's Burgers. The popular burger joint had the cleanest kitchen, as well as the best burgers in town. The owners kept up the place well, and I often ate lunch here when I worked at The Bends. As we walked inside and found a seat among the red booths, I wondered why the pack would meet here. Usually, we convened at my parents' home. A few families had gathered already, and many scarfed down the tantalizing fries and fire-grilled burgers.

I barely had the strength to sit without squeaking. My stomach grumbled, and Thorn rushed to put in our order before I tackled someone for their chow. By the time Thorn had made our order, Aggie and Brenna arrived to snag the other two seats on the opposite of my booth.

"Holy shit, you look awful." Aggie sighed. "Why do you always look like you got your ass handed to you?"

I flipped her off, then returned to my task of slowly using antibacterial wipes to clean off the condiment bottles on the table.

The earth witch tried not to laugh. "And I thought I was working on subtlety. Aggie, you got me beat."

"Something attacked me, and the pack is meeting tonight to talk about it," I explained.

"Again?" Aggie groaned.

It would've been nice to go the whole summer without an

incident, but when you were a supernatural creature, you got all the fun. Of course, humans had to deal with rush hour and bread running out during snowstorms, but this was quite different.

"Oh, Nat," Aggie added. "I know the dog shit has already hit the fan, but be on the lookout for a girls' night out in the future. I want to do a movie night as a housewarming."

I nodded, hoping things would quiet down so I could do *normal* things.

By the time Misty showed up with our tray of food, most of the humans had left and only werewolves remained. The Stravinskys in one corner were the noisiest lot, with Uncle Boris laughing louder than necessary. I wanted to go over and say hello to Mom, but I settled for a wave instead. Mom waved back with a concerned smile. I should expect another visit sooner rather than later.

Mom and Dad sat at a table with my aunts and uncles. Between the Stravinskys, my younger cousins chased each other until a stern eye from Mom got them to sit down at the kids' table nearby.

The order-up bell in the kitchen rang multiple times. Poor Misty would have her work cut out for her tonight with all these hungry pack members. Even her brother Jake, the cashier, offered a hand to get the orders out of the kitchen.

As everyone settled in, a final set of pack members entered the joint to stand in the back. Jake paused in the middle of delivering an order to get a glimpse of Erica Holden. She had that effect on others with her chiseled cheekbones, perfectly styled blonde hair, and refined charm. She gave me a respectful nod, and I returned the gesture. We had a long and tumultuous history, since she'd wanted to marry Thorn, but in the end, he chose me. After all that drama—and I didn't use the word *drama* lightly—we ended up working together at The Bends and had formed a truce of sorts. She had a strong work ethic and didn't take any shit from my coworkers.

I ignored the other new arrival. Rex floated into the joint with his chin held high. My younger cousins swooned at the sight of his handsome face, but I knew his heart was as empty as my dinner plate. Other than his desire to protect his younger brothers, I couldn't think of many redeeming qualities for him. Thorn and Rex had grown up together—and somehow, they ended up as best friends—but I never got the same treatment. Matter of fact, Rex took every opportunity to show me he'd caught the same asshole disease Farley contracted.

Instead of joining Erica in the back of the room, Rex stood next to Thorn. I didn't trust the man, but as Thorn told me once, we all had reasons why we did what we did.

"Good to see everyone," Thorn began. He strolled through the restaurant, touching shoulders and the top of the pups' heads. "I know this meeting came last minute, but we have another threat." Thorn recounted what I'd told him about the missing whistle, the fallen night guard, and my attack in Jake Branch County Park.

Murmurs flowed through the room while Jake and Misty continued to bring out food.

"This new predator sounds serious," Dad called out.

"It's dangerous," I added. I told them additional details about the prints I'd uncovered from a large humanoid creature and the paw prints.

A questioning gaze swept through the room. I searched their faces, too. Could one of us have stolen the whistle to call Cerberus and drive She Who Always Walks the Path away?

"Those two could be a problem, but why shouldn't we let them use the whistle?" Mom asked. "Wouldn't it benefit us?"

"Perhaps." All eyes turned to my father, the oldest werewolf in the room.

Dad continued, his voice rising. "Using magic comes with consequences. My family knows this very well. And if we use Cerberus's Dog Whistle, we should be prepared to hide as that mutt runs amok."

Rex snorted. "We're a pack, aren't we? Why should we fear a *dog* with multiple heads?" He took a step toward everyone with raised hands like he was the voice of reason. "We're stronger when we band together. I say we let the thief blow the whistle. If those thieves are smart, and I have a feeling they are, they'll use the dog whistle to drive that bitch away."

That got him a feminine chortle from the other side of the restaurant.

"You should tread lightly with things you don't understand," Brenna said, finally speaking up. "One of your people might get hurt or killed in the process. Have you met a twenty-foot-high, three-headed dog before?"

Rex's boastful grin melted off his face.

"I didn't think so," Brenna grumbled.

"*Mudak*," Uncle Boris mumbled in Russian.

That got a chuckle from my family. Even my uncle thought Rex was an asshole. He backed away to the wall and folded his arms.

"Seems like the best plan is to find the thieves and retrieve the whistle," Thorn said.

"If they haven't left the area yet," I added.

"The only way to know is to check," Thorn agreed.

"What about the spellcasters?" I shifted my attention to Brenna. "Trouble like this will bring them out of the weeds."

Brenna's brow furrowed. "I haven't heard anything from the respective spellcaster guilds, but if there's a possibility that someone will call Cerberus from his den, we're gonna have a *very* dangerous problem on our hands. We're talking about warlocks and wizards on every corner to contain its arrival."

My gaze connected with Thorn's. Determination flared in his hazel eyes. Like him, I was ready to do anything in my power to keep this situation under control before the pack faced grave peril.

CHAPTER 9

After everyone finished eating, parties formed to search the town and the surrounding environs. Naturally, I wasn't included. I had enough strength to shovel fries into my mouth, and that was about it. Now I had to return to the cottage and endure the marathon of westerns until Farley nodded off.

Thorn offered to take me home, but Brenna stepped up to drive me so he could join a search party.

"I'm done with my shift anyway," Brenna said. "Might as well escort you home, so you don't hurt yourself again."

If I didn't feel like a hot pile of garbage, I would've felt insulted. But I had no room to talk. I couldn't run with the pack in my current condition.

We left Archie's, and Brenna took her time. She even walked ahead of me to open the passenger door to her sunshine yellow VW Beetle.

"Still got your mom's car?" I said to make small talk.

"Yeah, I can't afford much else with my new pay." She shrugged. "Mama travels through jump points, so the car's just for show."

"What I wouldn't give for the ability to teleport," I grumbled. "Maybe I should spend the next couple of days in suspended animation like Han Solo."

"I think all you need is a couple nights of deep sleep," Brenna pointed out as she helped me sit. "If you were frozen like Han, you'd wake up in as much pain as you're in now."

"Good point." I relaxed against the leather seat. The faint scent of jasmine crossed my nose. "I really appreciate the ride. You didn't have to take me home; my parents could've taken me."

"I know." She adjusted the air conditioner vents to aim them in my direction, then she pulled out of the parking lot. "There are some things I didn't mention back at Archie's."

"Like what?" Spellcasters often held back to not frighten others. Nick did it to me all the time.

She frowned, revealing the deep dimple in her cheek. "I've known Dayla and Mimi were in town for a while now, but I'd hoped they'd sell their crap and leave without making trouble."

"Oh, really now. What else do you know about them? I've met a succubus before, but Mimi and Dayla aren't sex demons."

"They're something else entirely. Their kind usually keeps to themselves. Having not one, but two selling goods to humans is rare."

I nodded.

Brenna continued. "During my schooling, my elders taught me to tap into nature and draw strength from the elements. Some demons do the same, while others draw their power from other beings."

"And what about demons that eat people?"

Brenna didn't laugh. That wasn't a good sign. "You're not a source of sustenance to her, thank the heavens. If she ate wildlife, namely the human population, we would've noticed missing people already. She consumes something else."

"How dangerous are the demons?" I asked.

She sighed. "They're very dangerous, but in order to find out *how* dangerous they are, I'd have to meet her."

"She isn't blocking you, is she?" Maybe Mimi masked herself in other ways.

"I could walk in there and buy whatever I want, but I'm not stupid enough to attempt a read and get myself killed. We're taught from a young age to avoid demons unless absolutely necessary. Some of them are unpredictable, and you don't know if you're messing with a nuclear bomb until you're messing around with the buttons."

Brenna's insight didn't surprise me. The fear I'd felt was real. The wolf within me recognized the night demon as a fellow predator.

Briefly, I let myself close my eyes and said, "Essentially, you're saying it's in our best interest to find the whistle and return it to her."

"Pretty much."

Soon enough, we pulled up to the cottage. Right as I was getting comfortable.

"Last question," I said. "I know you're not sure how powerful Dayla and Mimi are, but I have to think ahead. I need to protect the pack. If we fail to find the whistle, will the pack have to leave the area?"

She snorted. "I wouldn't leave the area. I'd add a *couple* of states between me and her if I was you."

With Brenna's intel, I entered the house feeling even more tired. I could already hear the loud television as Brenna trailed after me into the foyer. Not far from us, Farley lounged on the La-Z-Boy, perfectly content with a bag of Lay's chips in one hand and a Pabst Blue Ribbon in the other.

I didn't dare look at the floor around him.

"Good evening," Brenna called out politely.

Farley grunted.

As she helped me into bed, I asked her the one thing I knew she wouldn't mind telling me. "Nick has to spend some time in a free warlock clinic as an exercise for Dr. Frank. Did he tell you anything about it?"

She rolled her eyes. "I've known about it for a long time." She pushed her short hair behind her ear. "I've tried to bring up the subject, but he won't talk about it."

"Any ideas on how I can help him?" I asked. "He ignored the text I sent him about meeting up."

Now that got a smile out of the earth witch. "I'll be happy to offer a hand. When you're ready to meet him, shoot me a text."

Glad to have a co-conspirator, I asked, "Why does he need to spend time at the clinic? I thought he already knew how to heal people?"

Her face softened. "That's Nick's tale to tell, I'm afraid. What I can say is that avoiding this exercise won't help him."

"So, you're saying he's at a standstill." I yawned and cringed from expanding my chest too quickly.

"More or less." She glanced at the empty glass next to the bed. "Want me to get you something to drink?"

"Sure, it's going to be a long night with all that noise." I gestured to the far wall. "I haven't slept well."

With a sympathetic nod, Brenna left the room. Ten minutes later, she returned.

"Did you have to draw the water from a nearby well?" I joked.

She presented a tall glass with a blended dark green fluid that smelled like fresh fruit and herbs like parsley and ginger.

"That looks like the smoothies they sell at the malt shop," I remarked.

"Drink up." She winked at me.

After one sip, I grinned like a fool. It was quite good. Briefly, I wondered how she'd gathered, cut up, and blended everything, but I was too tired to care. Maybe she hid fruit and such in deep magical pockets like Nick's. I chugged down the rest. Ten seconds later, a delicious hum fluttered through my belly. The room around me grew fuzzy, but I didn't mind. Even the wolf within me rolled over and surrendered. I joined it and settled into the wonders of oblivion.

CHAPTER 10

For the first time in months, I woke up feeling like a freshly unwrapped Christmas present. I felt joyful, sparkling, and ready to kick some ass—even with that television still blaring in the other room. A quick peek at my phone revealed not only had I gotten a good night's sleep, but I'd managed a good *forty-eight hours'* worth.

I poked my mate next to me. "Did Brenna tell you how long I'd sleep?"

Thorn's head rose and he blinked. His blond hair stuck up in odd directions. "Yeah, she left a note. The healer came by and said you needed the rest."

"Two days of rest?" I couldn't resist chuckling.

"Believe me, it was good you slept. Especially, when we changed your dressings. The debridement was kinda gross."

I shuddered and tried to bury thoughts of my decaying flesh. "Did any of it leak on the bed?"

He drew in a deep breath. That would be a yes. "Whatever hit you obliterated the top layers of your skin. Those layers died and sloughed off—"

"Yeah, don't tell me." I slipped out of the bed. I'd worry

about the mattress's condition another day. "What happened while I was out? Did the pack find anything?"

He sat up. Exhaustion lined his face. "Not a thing. A rainstorm went through the area and destroyed the tracks. Without a scent or footprints, we ran blind and found nothing."

He added, "We plan to try again this weekend."

I nodded then kissed his cheek. "I'd hoped for better news, but we still have time. Why don't you get some rest? I'll make some breakfast."

His hazel eyes darkened to molten gold as he reached for my hand and tried to tug me back to bed. "Or we could *snuggle* some more. You only drooled a little."

"Comments like that won't earn you a snuggle-buddy."

He laughed. It was good to see the easy smile that set my heart aflutter. Thorn released me and placed a pillow over his head. "Thirty more minutes then. I'll be up soon."

"Uh, huh. I don't know how you sleep through that TV." I threw on a *Santa's Little Helper* T-shirt and bright red shorts. It felt good to accomplish something as simple as putting on clothes.

Thorn released a long sigh. "I grew up with the noise. It's like one of those rain machines now."

Like a rain machine? Yeah, not in this lifetime.

I plodded out of the bedroom and through the hallway to the living room. I expected to find Farley enjoying his breakfast with a side of Old West justice, but the La-Z-Boy was empty and the door to the second bedroom closed.

Lovely.

I picked up the remote and jabbed my finger on the OFF button. How hard would it be to turn off the TV? Wouldn't that lower our power bill this month? Hell, maybe he could turn it off and help everyone get a good night's sleep? I stared hard at Farley's door and tried to think of *any* reason why I should buy that man a gift.

I couldn't think of any.

Grandma Lasovskaya would want me to respect my elders no matter the situation, but should I let him disrespect me in the process?

Now that I'd turned off the TV, I couldn't resist peeking around the recliner. God help me, it was a shit show. There was not one, but many old, shriveled, and stale dill and pickle potato chips between my toes. I shuffled a step to the left and found beer nuts scattered like bird seed across the living room. I stooped to pick up a couple nuts, then I gave in to let the cleaning bug hit. My poor empty stomach protested, but I grabbed my handheld vacuum cleaner and circled the La-Z-Boy.

Thorn peeked around the corner to investigate the noise. Once he saw me working, he murmured an apology, then disappeared again. My mate knew better than to interfere when I went into cleaning-mode.

By the time the vacuum had sucked up the decomposing debris around the armchair, the furniture almost looked brand-new. Well, minus the nacho cheese stains on the armrest, the stickiness from soda spills in one spot, and the greasy hair gel imprint on the headrest.

Other than *those* things, I had my chair back.

Instead of losing my entire morning to deep cleaning the chair with a steam attachment on my vacuum, I made myself proud. I thought outside of the box and found the large piece of plastic I used to protect my furniture while I painted. After I covered the recliner, I breathed a sigh of relief.

Now all is right with the world.

Sadly, the moment that man left this house, I'd jettison that chair into orbit and I'd never have to see those stains again.

Time to stuff my face with some chow. I walked into the kitchen to find the next mess: plates with crusted-on food piled on the counter, a tipped over container of beer nuts on the kitchenette table, and the worst offense of them all: someone had used the washcloth for the dishes to cover a spill on the linoleum floor.

Let's not talk about the fact that the spill was still there.

I walked around the puddle and opened the fridge. Eat first. Then go nuclear.

There was nothing left to eat except the *seledka pod shuboi* my aunt brought a couple days ago. No TV dinners, milk, or fresh vegetables. No deli meat either.

But there was plenty of unopened beer to join the beer bottles on the counter.

I yanked out the casserole container and even snagged a beer too. Might as well start happy hour before I put on my hazmat suit. I grabbed a big spoon, laid a fresh towel over one of the kitchen seats, and then sat. No one bothered me as I shoveled the food into my mouth. The beer went down nicely too.

At least Farley had good taste in alcohol.

The food filled my stomach, but other problems remained.

Not long into eating, my phone dinged with a new text. The hairs on the back of my neck rose. That was never a good sign. I checked the screen to see a text from *Unknown.* The message read: *Another artifact was taken last night. It was a beaded jade bracelet used to protect the wearer from incredible heat.*

My hand shook, but I held the phone tightly.

Based on the message, I had no doubt that Mademoiselle Midnight had reached out to text me, and whoever was behind these thefts had sinister plans that might end with the death of everyone I cared for.

CHAPTER 11

Somehow, I had to find the whistle. I could spend the day searching through the parks, but in the end, I'd run in circles like the pack. What I needed to do was check the next potential thief: the spring fairy vacationing in Manhattan. How I'd find her was the next question.

I shot Brenna a text: *Please tell the wizard I want to meet him today.*

Five minutes later, the phone dinged with a reply: *No need to tell him. Nick Fenton will conveniently be at Earl's Fine Antiques at 11:30 am.*

Having Brenna as a co-conspirator to corner Nick was one of my better ideas. After I slipped into my blouse and pencil skirt, I escaped the house to Brooklyn and arrived at eleven-twenty. Ten minutes later, from my hiding spot in the diner across the street from Earl's place, I was pleasantly surprised to see my target stroll inside right at thirty minutes past eleven.

Right as I planned to dart across the street, my phone dinged with a new text message from Aggie: *Movie night tonight at seven! Since you don't have a job, your unemployed ass better show up. I will hunt you down if you don't.*

Guess I had plans tonight.

I made my way across the busy Brooklyn street and darted toward Earl's Fine Antiques. The place had an old wooden storefront with an awning covering the sidewalk. Two large, junk-filled bins sat in front of the single window-pane. During every visit, I wondered if leaving containers out there on the sidewalk was just begging people to come by and steal them, but the owner had placed a protective ward on the bins. Quite clever, if you asked me. The heavy scent of cinnamon, a tell-tale sign of a spellcaster's magic left me wary, so I hurried inside.

Based on my past excursions with Nick into this establishment, we both loved browsing here. Every time I walked over the threshold, a honeyed feeling tickled my stomach. I wanted to find something new. A potential holiday gem to add to my forever-growing collection. And as much as I wasn't fond of buying Farley anything other than a broom, a mop, and a bib, it wouldn't hurt for me to try to uncover something that might shave down the bristles on that man's backside. Maybe he'd even thank me.

I navigated my way through the first set of displays with well-cared for Victorian and medieval furniture with ease. Fine leatherback books lined the far wall, while a tall table nearby had small glass goblets full of bubbling potions. It was once I snuck past two glass display cases with shimmering jewelry that I spotted my target.

Nick faced away from me, but he still said, "How did you know I'd be here?" He sighed. "Don't tell me. Brenna?"

"She wanted to help us finish our group therapy exercise."

He laughed a bit. "If it wasn't one of Dr. Frank's treatment plans, Brenna would've told you to drag me where I needed to go."

Nick turned around and I finally noticed what he held in his hands: a set of well-preserved Victorian-era paper ornaments arranged in an enclosed frame. My fingertips tingled at the sight of the delicate snowflakes, a blushing paper doll, and five-pointed stars. I could faintly make out the faded music sheets the original crafter had used.

"Oh, I don't have any of those," I remarked, but I forced myself to step back. "You're not going to ensnare me with that, buddy." I took the frame, admired it briefly, then put it down. "How come you haven't replied to any of my texts? I thought we were friends."

"We are friends. We always will be." He paused and stared out the shop window to the busy street. "Right now, I need to fix myself and heal other spellcasters, but I can't bring myself to do it."

I scoffed. Always the hero, white wizards tended to have do-gooder complexes. If I truly thought about it, that had to be tiring. Even I had days when I didn't want to bail the goblin out of trouble at The Bends.

I wanted to know if Nick had any intel on the spring fairies, but we had other business to handle. "Dr. Frank said he wanted you to volunteer at a free clinic, right?"

"Yeah, he wants me to face a similar situation to the one that got me in trouble in the first place."

I took a moment to pause. "Is what happened at medical school related to treating another spellcaster?"

Ever since Nick had returned from medical school, I'd wanted to know how to help my dear friend. My invites to hang out or chat had gone without a reply.

Nick went quiet on me until we left the antique store and walked a block or two down the street. Cars zipped by and families strolled past us, but we took our time until he ended the silence. "I made a grave error with an important patient."

My heart faltered. "I'm sorry about that. What happened?"

We crossed another street.

"When I first arrived, I learned I had a lot more field experience than other students. Many of them came from highborn wizard families. They had decades of study through private tutors and some had even attended a prestigious university or two." He sighed. "I, on the other hand, came only with a burning desire to comfort the sick, to fix what was broken."

We veered to the east to head into the shade in Prospect Park. I welcomed the trees overhead.

Nick continued. "I also had Dr. Frank's recommendation and that came with a burden I wasn't prepared to bear."

"I had no idea our therapist carried such weight in the magical community either."

"When I showed up to my classes, the teachers had high expectations. They gave me more difficult assignments. In the beginning, I carried the burden well, but over time the cracks appeared. When I thought no one was looking, I started picking up rocks and other shiny things I found on the ground. At first, I believed my trips along the quiet streets in Budapest were a part of a new healthy habit to clear my mind, but when one of my wizard pockets began to fill with random things, I realized I had a growing anxiety problem." He briefly closed his eyes. "I had more than a couple of rocks in my pockets."

My tongue thickened in my mouth. His shame touched me deeply. "You were excessively hoarding again?"

He nodded. "And my stress carried over into patient treatment, too. After transferring a witch's eczema from her hands to her face, I got my first strike. Then I spread a warlock's genital warts across his forehead. Strike two.

Somehow, I clawed my way to my finals for the semester, but I failed in the end."

Nick stopped in the middle of the sidewalk. "I nearly killed my patient."

Other pedestrians veered around us. For once in a long time, I could hear my friend's racing heart. I could feel his regret seeping from his pores. Usually, he blocked those sounds from me.

"My professor had to resuscitate them when I *refused* to intervene," he said, his voice hollow. "Sounds crazy, huh?"

I took Nick's hand and waited until his heart slowed down again. When the moment passed, I sighed for both of us.

"You don't sound crazy," I said. "You're one of the strongest people I know. Matter of fact, since you've returned from overseas you've done a great job helping my family."

"Your family doesn't have any expectations like my people."

"True." I tugged him forward a bit, then released his hand when he followed. "Dr. Frank would tell us to confront what we fear and expose ourselves to it over and over again. We could walk by the clinic, and not go inside today, if that would make you feel like you're trying?"

He considered my suggestion and nodded. "Seems easy enough."

We left the shelter of the park out into the heat again. Two jump points later, we left Brooklyn and arrived outside of a four-story brownstone on the Upper East Side. A woman and her child passed us, but other than that, we were alone on this side of the street.

"Is the clinic usually this busy?" I joked.

"It's busy enough. Most patients use a glamour or a direct jump point inside the office."

"Sounds convenient." My small talk died off. A part of me hoped coming this close would entice him to want to go inside, but he didn't.

Maybe we needed a couple more trips.

"I'm thirsty," I said offhand. "Let's find a street vendor."

As we left the front of the clinic, he admitted, "I don't know why I'm hesitating. Or why I didn't call you to seek help. Maybe I didn't reply to your texts because I didn't want to bother you. Yeah, I know that sounds like an excuse, but you've got your own life in Jersey now. You've got a husband and a huge family to support you. I wouldn't want you worrying about me when you've got enough problems of your own."

If he only knew. "You should always reach out to your friends," I said firmly. "And yes, I've got problems, but I want to be there for you, too. If we have to setup lawn chairs in front of this place, we'll do it." I scratched my head while I considered my limited free time.

"I really appreciate it." He finally flashed me the half-smile I missed. "Do you have to return home to get ready for work?"

"About that…" I told Nick about my horrible start at the night demon's ceramic mart, the dead night guard, and my subsequent attack. I didn't want his help to find the fairies, but if he knew anything, I'd welcome any suggestions.

"Why didn't you tell me you'd gotten hurt? That's not a problem, that's…a lot worse."

"No shit. Like you said, we both have *a lot* going on." I circled and showed him I was fine. "I'm good to go, but I need to find the spring fairies. They might have the whistle, and if I can get close enough, I might be able to see it through magic."

"I have no idea how to find them," Nick admitted. "They

usually keep to themselves and avoid spellcasters. Did the night demon give any hints where they might be staying?"

"None."

Nick thought a bit. "My boss back at the antique store in East Village might have info we could use. He takes specialty orders from Old Land tourists." Nick pulled out his cell phone and send a rapid text.

Ten minutes later, after we'd snagged some cool drinks, we got the information I badly needed.

"We need to go downtown," Nick explained. "My boss said the Winter Court likes the Time Square Marriott Hotel while the Summer Court avoids them and vacations in the Hamptons. The Spring Court can't stand the Summer Court, so they stay at the Four Seasons off E 57th." He chuckled. "You got that?"

Geez. And I thought I had familial issues.

Nick's phone beeped again. He read the phone and added, "If you're patient, you should be able to catch them during their teatime around twelve-thirty. I've had weird orders of tea sets sent there."

I tilted my head. "Care to crash a tea party with me?"

His smile widened. "That sounds a lot more fun than what I had planned this afternoon."

"More shopping?" I quipped.

"Maybe." He chuckled a little.

Since we didn't have much time before twelve-thirty, Nick and I hurried west across Manhattan to the Four Seasons. Using a nearby jump point, Nick tossed us into a basement storage room at the hotel.

"Not bad, Fenton." The pitch-black room we arrived in smelled a bit musty and dusty, but at least we landed in a clean spot without any creepy creatures guarding it. "Glad to see a jump point here."

Nick retrieved an oak staff from one of the magical

pockets in his black coat. The tip of the staff brightened to illuminate the dark corners of the room. "The fairies leave magical traces wherever they congregate frequently."

We weaved our way around stacks of dusty chairs and folded up tables.

"Over the last fifty years," Nick added, "wizards and warlocks tapped into their signal, you might say."

"Like a beacon?"

"You could call it that, but, like I said, my people don't associate with fairies often. There's been too much of a sordid history between warlocks and the fairy folk."

I gestured to his beautiful staff. "Will the spring fairies attack first and ask questions later?"

"Hope not."

"They'll probably have guards since they were attacked not too long ago." I didn't want to fight them either, but I had to be prepared.

With Nick's help to mask our presence, we snuck out of the basement, then hurried through a set of staircases until we reached the main floor. Locked doors slowed us down here and there, but Nick got us through all of them.

After navigating through the main halls, we eventually found the signs for upcoming events. One in particular, hosted in the private Westgate Ballroom, piqued my attention: *Spring Court Party*.

That got a snort out of me. "Why not come up with something less obvious?"

He shrugged. "If a human walked in, they'd see nothing but a bunch of other humans eating. Why bother pretending? They're vacationing among humans for a reason."

The double doors to the Westgate Ballroom were closed, but I cracked them open to peek inside. About fifty fairies used half the ballroom to have their meal of decadent tea cakes, scones, and fresh Earl Grey tea near the expansive windows overlooking E 57th Street. Fairy guards dressed in black suits surrounded them at a respectful distance.

I took a deep breath before I walked inside, but one fairy in particular stopped me cold. An elfin child with short, dark hair sat at the far end of the room. She stood out from everyone else in her bright red coat with large buttons down the front, a pair of white tights, and black Mary Jane shoes. Her legs were crossed, and she munched on a tea cake with dainty bites. Others enjoyed their food around her, including my target, Lady Ophelia.

Thank goodness, I'd found her, but I'd run into someone I'd hoped not to see for a long time.

My hand tightened on the doorknob. I had to make a decision. We couldn't stand here for long, but I couldn't stop staring at Lisbetta, the child queen of the Spring Court. Visions of her feeding off werewolves flooded through me. That child had stopped bullets from AK-47s, and she'd used magic to toss around objects with ease.

If I closed my eyes, I could still see the night she'd taken down her enemies: Her tiny form swarmed on them, leaping on one attacker to another. When she touched them, they folded in on themselves and withered away. Bodies convulsed from her grasp.

"What do you want to do?" Nick whispered, interrupting the flood of memories.

My mind screamed at me to turn around and go home, but I forced myself to open the door. "I have to know if they have the whistle."

I walked in and Nick tried to grasp my wrist but missed. As much as I wanted to add a couple of counties between Lisbetta and myself, I had to speak with Lady Ophelia.

My pack depended on this conversation.

A hush fell over the room and all eyes landed on Nick and

me as we approached the guards. The menacing fairies tight-ened the gaps between them to keep us from passing.

"You're not welcome here, Wolf," a tall fairy with dark eyes intoned.

"Looks like a great tea party, but I need to speak with one of your ladies." I kept my distance yet glanced at Ophelia. The lady in question ignored me and kept speaking to the companion next to her about shopping in Miami this fall.

I dared not look at the young fairy queen, but I caught her smiling at me from the corner of my eye.

"Long time no see, Little Wolf," she called out sweetly with a smile. "Let her come closer."

The guards parted and a small group of fairies escorted us. None of them brandished weapons, but I suspected they had hidden ones. We got within ten feet of the party. Court ladies stared at us with concern. It was likely none of them had expected a wizard and a wolf to crash their teatime.

My gaze flicked to Lisbetta's gloved hands, but I forced myself to return the smile and take in her face. "Hello, your Majesty. Sorry to disturb your gathering, but I came to speak with one of your sisters about an important matter."

"Who might that be?" she asked.

"Lady Ophelia," I replied.

"How interesting." Lisbetta swung her feet and picked up another finger sandwich from a nearby platter. She turned to Lady Ophelia. "What business does the wolf have with you today?"

My former customer's face grew pale. "Before you arrived a couple of days ago to protect us, many wicked creatures attacked the Spring Court. A creature we haven't identified yet killed one of my ladies-in-waiting."

"I'm sorry to hear about that," I said gently. "What shape was she in, if you don't mind me asking?"

"An animal with claws and teeth had gutted her," she

replied. "What was even more strange, the animal had left what looked like burns around her wounds."

So these creatures were the same ones that had attacked me two days ago.

Lisbetta paused in the middle of eating. Had this news not been revealed to her?

Lady Ophelia continued. "I...took it upon myself to see the night demon about a weapon to protect us, your Majesty."

"Did you now?" Lisbetta put down her sandwich and wiped off her mouth with a dainty light blue napkin.

Nick and I took a step back. My mother only said that term when she wasn't amused.

Lady Ophelia smiled so hard that her cheek twitched. "One of my girls received an advertisement for the night demon's barge, and I thought using Cerberus's whistle would drive away our pursuers. When the night demon refused to sell it to me, I tried to sneak on the ship and failed—"

"You did what?" Lisbetta asked.

Nick and I backed up again. If Ophelia had had a Russian mother's love (also known as upbringing), she'd start apologizing now instead of later.

Ophelia's right hand shook, and her lower lip trembled. "I tried again a couple hours later and managed to steal the night demon's whistle."

Lisbetta and I exchanged a glance. I wasn't sure what the young queen thought, but at least I knew who'd taken the whistle.

But how did the two set of prints I discovered around the night guard play into all this?

"You said you failed the first time," I said. "Did the night guard stop you?"

"That cretin tossed me overboard like I was trash," Ophelia replied stiffly.

"But you returned later?" I asked.

She nodded. "I had to have it, so I tried again not long before the sun rose. The night guard was gone, so I took a chance and stole the whistle."

Damn, so that's how all this went down.

My attackers took out the night guard for some reason, then Lady Ophelia was able to snatch the goods.

"I even left spiritual currency to pay for it," Lady Ophelia snapped. "Doesn't that count?"

I snorted and shook my head, recalling how I ended up working for the demons after doing the *same* thing at Kramkar's thrift store.

Even after Lady Ophelia's explanation, I still had unanswered questions about who'd attacked me and killed the night guard, but at least I could get the whistle back. I extended my hand. "My pack would've gotten into huge trouble if I hadn't found you. I need to return the whistle to Mademoiselle Midnight. If you want, I'll even get your money back."

She stared at my hand, and I recognized her expression before she said a thing. Her brow furrowed and the grimace on her face practically advertised that she didn't have the damn thing anymore.

"Where is it?" I asked slowly. "Please don't tell me you gave it to someone else."

"I didn't give it away," she admitted. She mumbled words even I couldn't hear, and the other fairies in the room snickered. One dark look from Lisbetta silenced them.

"It was stolen." Lady Ophelia's voice rose to a painful pitch. "A leprechaun mugged me in Central Park."

I was so screwed.

Lisbetta's head snapped in Ophelia's direction. The queen spoke to her subject in a tongue I didn't recognize. Ophelia lowered her head farther.

"Since my subject decided to protect the court herself," Lisbetta said, "I commend her actions. What I don't like is how she *stole* property from a demon and brought Little Wolf into this mess. Unfortunately, we are in your debt and must make this right."

The Spring Queen beckoned me closer. I reluctantly shuffled forward, and Nick caught my arm.

No, his dark eyes conveyed.

"Don't worry, Wizard," Lisbetta purred. "I had quite the feast this spring."

Nick released me, and I approached the child queen. Up close, she smelled like a field of poppies and tulips I wanted to disappear within. The wolf within me relaxed while the human quaked on the outside.

"We never should've angered the night demon." The queen slowly shook her head. "Did she tell you when she wanted it back?"

"She gave me two weeks," I replied. "Four of those days have passed already."

"Then we don't have much time."

Since I had the queen's attention, I said, "The creatures that attacked your court also stole an artifact from the Midnight Barge. It will protect them from great heat. Do you have any ideas what it could be? An old enemy?"

"I don't know right now, but I'll let you know if I learn anything," she replied.

I added a curtsy to thank her for *not* eating me. "Thank you, your Majesty."

"And you." The child's gaze flicked to Lady Ophelia. "You will help Little Wolf and the wizard search every leprechaun pawn shop until dusk."

Lady Ophelia hid her distaste well, but she clasped her hands together until the knuckles turned white.

"Why should we search the pawn shops?" I asked.

"Leprechauns only live and die for money," Lisbetta said with a small frown. "You'll most certainly recover your whistle if you search their shops."

I thanked her again. "Be mindful, your Majesty. Whatever attacked your court is still out there."

"I hope they come for us." Her frown blossomed into a grin. "I'd make room for a worthy meal before my bedtime."

CHAPTER 12

Unrelenting July heat bounced off the cement and baked my shoulders as we searched for the whistle. Beside me, Nick barely broke out in a sweat.

"Someday, I want to learn a spell like the one you got in your coat," I said to him.

He chuckled as we walked with Lady Ophelia to the fourth supernatural pawn shop in Queens.

"You can borrow it, if you're too hot," he offered.

"No, I'm fine as long as I stick to the shade." I wiped my damp brow with the back of my hand. "By the way, you don't have to help us all day. I feel bad dragging you around."

"I wouldn't stay unless I wanted to help," he said sternly. "To be honest, I could use a couple distractions right now, and Brenna would give me an earful if I abandoned you. Your Spring Court friend isn't much help."

We turned around to see the lady in question followed us a few paces behind. With each visit to a shop, she hadn't said much. A mumble here or there to ask a leery leprechaun behind the counter if they had what we wanted. We would've been better off if she'd stayed behind at the hotel.

"How many more in this neighborhood?" I took a long drink from a water bottle. Properly hydrated, I could shop all day.

"At least two more," Nick replied.

To tug Ophelia back into the mix, I asked her a question that came to mind as we pounded the pavement. "You had the whistle for a couple of hours, right?"

We finally approached the next shop. O'Malley's Pawn and Jewelry probably didn't have it either.

"A couple of hours, yes," she replied sourly.

"Why didn't you blow it once you had it?"

"I was scared what would happen if I did," she admitted. "Fairy children learn legends about the creatures outside of the Old World at a young age. Especially the tales of about Cerberus and Hercules. We learned how the great hero captured it from Hades' realm and restrained it in the mortal world with the help of Hermes through a mysterious whistle. Anyone who blows it can summon the beast to do their bidding for one task."

"I see." I stopped right outside the door to finish our conversation.

"As much as I wanted to protect us," she said, "I realized once I let the 'dog' out of the bag, as you humans say, I wouldn't be able to restrain the animal again."

"Yeah, a twenty-foot dog running rampant in Manhattan would be problematic." I ventured into the pawn shop first, and the others followed.

The rattling air conditioner against the wall belted out more heat than cool air. The whole place smelled musty and questionable, like my brother's sports bag from when he played football in high school. There wasn't much to the pawn shop, like the last couple of establishments. Wall-to-wall glass displays kept sticky fingers from handling an assortment of jewelry, weapons, and exotic goods.

This joint was a hot mess. Whoever worked here hadn't sorted out the stock. An eighteenth-century travel vanity sat next to a set of 1970s bow ties. Not far from that, dollar-store pearl earrings were placed above a priceless Olmec woven handbasket. The itch to rearrange everything practically smacked me in the face.

At the far end of the narrow shop, tucked among the mishmash of goods, a leprechaun greeted us. As we got closer, I spied a wall of bullet-resistant glass in front of the pale fellow with ruddy cheeks and a reddish five o'clock shadow across his chin. He wore a fancy black dress shirt and dark gray vest. The leprechaun had unfastened three buttons on his shirt to reveal a pelt of curly, dark red chest hair. And boy, did he have a lot of chest hair. I was a were-wolf who could appreciate a hairy chest, but the leprechaun looked as though a wild animal sought to escape the confines of his shirt.

"See something you like?" the leprechaun added.

With one squint, I glimpsed the creature hidden under-neath the glamour. He stood at the height of my waist, and his ginger curls appeared smoothed back with a foul-smelling gel. The real leprechaun smiled at me, revealing oversized chompers.

"We're looking for a special whistle." Nick specified the size with the span of his stretched-out hands.

"Been a while since a wizard walked through the door." The leprechaun pulled a Kool cigarette from his pocket, lit the end with a brass lighter, then took a long drag. "Usually, I only get warlocks," he said as he blew out the smoke.

For some reason, the cigarette smoke didn't cross my nose. What other secrets did this creature keep?

"I see," Nick said carefully.

"What's your name, Wizard?" the leprechaun asked.

"My name doesn't matter." Nick's face resembled stone. "Why don't you give us yours?"

The store owner flicked ash off the cigarette's end. "Seamus is the name."

"That's a fine name," Nick said, carefully drawing him into a polite conversation. "Did one of your people bring a whistle by?"

That got us a greasy smile from the leprechaun. "If I have your little toy, are you interested in buying it?"

"I'll pay—" Ophelia began, but I grabbed her arm.

"That depends on whether you got it or not," I said.

After dealing with conniving goblins for years, I had a feeling the leprechauns doubled their prices too. Profit margins above honor.

Nick and I approached the seller. I swept my gaze over the shiny baubles and jewelry in the case in front of us, but I couldn't find the whistle. Did he keep it in the back, maybe?

Disappointment flicked at me, but in the corner of my eye, metal from an antique winked at me. One glimpse, and I knew I'd found a gem: a pristine .36-caliber 1851 Colt Navy Revolver. And not a stitch of glamor stuck to it, either. With its signature round hand guard and a small cut under the barrel for the paper cartridge, it was the real deal.

Would Farley like that? He watched westerns every day, and ammo wouldn't be important, since werewolves were forbidden to use weapons.

"Show us the whistle and we'll talk about compensation," Nick said, drawing my attention back to our mission.

"I don't know if I should do that," Seamus said smoothly. "The minute I pull it out, what's to stop you from taking it from me?"

That got a laugh from me. I blew against the glass and condensation didn't form. Matter of fact, my breath didn't bounce back at me either. "You're not really here, Seamus."

He gave me an appreciative nod. "No, I'm not, sweet lady. And I must admit, your voice is sweeter than mince pie." He gave me the sleaziest look-over I'd ever seen.

Even the spring fairy shuddered.

"I might sound sweet," I said, "but I'm not that pretty once a month. Look, I'm tired, hungry, and I'd like to go home. Do you have the whistle or not?"

"I don't have it," he admitted with an apologetic grin, "but I might be able to find it for you, if you're interested in working for me?"

"Working for you?" I already technically had two jobs now. Working in this pawn shop would be an easy no. "Not interested."

"Nat—" Nick began.

"You wouldn't be working in this hot box." Seamus's grin became as slippery as bacon sliding across a pan. "You could make some money with my other ladies. They like to chat and *make* friends with our customers. And I'm a strong man. I'll give you all the protection you'll need."

I about choked on my spit. *He's a pimp.*

"We don't need your help," Nick said firmly. "Nat, we should leave."

Something tickled the back of my neck as Seamus murmured words I couldn't hear. The compulsion to step forward slammed into me until Nick blocked my path.

"That's enough, leprechaun." Nick's dark eyes flashed bright enough for me to turn away. "Or do we need to settle this the old-fashioned way in the remote realm you're hiding in?"

With that warning, Seamus backed off and the compulsion disappeared. "I was just being friendly."

Friendly, my hairy ass.

"Nat, let's go," Ophelia said.

I turned to leave, but before I changed my mind, I

couldn't resist asking one more question. "Is that Colt Navy Revolver for sale?"

"Yes, it is," Seamus said with little interest. "Will that be a charge or cash?"

~

I should've felt tired after searching through those hot pawn shops, but I actually had a skip in my step. Aggie's invite to her housewarming movie night helped. Maybe binging a couple of movies would lift my spirits. I hadn't been able to spend quality time with her to catch up on things either.

On the way to Aggie's apartment, I stopped at the local market to pick up a few of her favorites. Her fridge might be empty by now—might as well stuff her pantry with the delights.

Once I arrived, I hurried up the steps toward her apartment, but as I reached the door, a familiar scent crossed my nose. I raised my hand to knock but hesitated. I knew that light, yet expensive perfume all too well. Erica Holden had stood here recently.

Before I could escape, Aggie opened the door.

"There you are, Sunshine," she said smugly. She snatched the grocery bag with one hand and grabbed my wrist with the other. "I was wondering what was taking you so long, but I can see your brought something far better than DVDs."

She tugged me into the apartment. Fresh chili bubbled in a pot in the kitchen, while on the other side of the room, Erica sat in one of the chairs nibbling on popcorn.

"Hey, Nat." My former rival gave me a tentative smile. "Good to see you up and about."

I gave her a nod. We hadn't chatted since I'd begun my stint working at the demon's place. Of course, we spoke at work about menial things, like keeping the fire witch from burning the place down, or complaining about Bill's bad habits. Basically, work stuff.

When it came to personal matters, we avoided those. Especially after the heart-to-heart we had before we found out it was her father who'd worked with the Basilisk King.

Now that we were about to have dinner and watch a movie together, I couldn't help but think about the words she'd said not too long ago. "Maybe if I spend more time with you, I'll understand you better. And maybe I'll become a better person, too."

Hanging out together sounded wise, but Erica had hurt me. Maybe my hesitation meant I wasn't as ready to spend time with her as she was with me.

Aggie directed me to sit across from Erica, while Aggie sat on the couch between us.

"You've done a good job decorating," I said.

She'd made the place cozy, but my seat felt as comfortable as a bed of thorns.

"Thanks—I'm still looking for a bedspread set," Aggie replied, "but Erica offered to give me one of hers."

"Oh, really." I nodded. Why hadn't Aggie asked me if I had any? Hell, I had one blanket with a delightful amount of holiday cheer. I'd considered bringing it by, but as I took in Aggie's new home with the splashes of navy blue, royal purple, and lavender, I realized my bedspread would've clashed with her decor.

"The chili's almost done," Aggie chirped, "but we should watch a show first. Maybe one of those reality shows the humans gossip about."

"Yes, we should," Erica gushed. "Did you hear about that show where people marry their partner at first sight?"

Aggie's face lit up. "Yes, it's a train wreck, but it's so good. My customers won't stop buzzing about it."

I tried to smile and failed. I'd heard of it, but I'd witnessed enough train wrecks over the last couple of days. I also didn't have a great history with arranged marriages. The day my parents tried to hook me up with Rex came to mind. Those kinds of hookups didn't have happy endings.

Aggie turned down the lights in the living room, and soon enough the TV glowed with the latest episode. Then the gossip started, and I had no idea what was going on. Aggie tried to pull me by my scruff into the conversation, but I didn't know any of the characters.

"Shouldn't someone check on the chili?" I offered.

"If you move from that seat, I'm going to kick your ass," Aggie snapped. "You're my guest."

Not long after her threat, she returned to the discussion at hand. "If Craig tells his wife he only plans to stay married because she's got a bangin' body again, I'm gonna snatch his scrawny neck through the screen and rip his throat out."

"He wouldn't try that shit with a werewolf," Erica added.

"The show would be over in one episode." Aggie cackled.

They both broke out into laughter, and I couldn't resist giggling with them. After what had happened with her ex-husband, it was good to see Aggie smiling again. Even her breakup with Will had affected her, but now Aggie glowed again.

My gaze flicked to Erica. She appeared relaxed…and receptive. When our gazes connected, instead of the resentment I used to see, she tilted her head with concern. "You okay, Nat?"

As a werewolf, I couldn't lie to these two when asked a direct question, so I settled for an explanation that conveyed what I felt. "I'm completely lost."

Aggie hit pause. "Sorry, Nat. So much has happened." She turned to Erica. "We need to go back to the beginning."

Oh, God, not more episodes.

My best friend continued. "She needs to see Craig's face when he meets Laura. Especially when she walks down the aisle. He wanted to unwrap her like a brand-new Butterfinger."

Aggie launched into an avalanche of more information than I wanted to know: Craig's background, Laura's favorite spot for romantic dinners, his sordid past with pole dancers who left him since he was a schmuck. For the next half-hour, I learned much more than I wanted to know about any flawed human relationship.

Once Aggie wrapped up her endless recap, I asked, "And these are real people and not actors?"

"Humans are just as jacked up as werewolves." Aggie shook her head with pursed lips. "Okay, I'm starving…again."

Aggie doled out the chili, and we settled in to watch a movie I hadn't seen in a while, *Pretty in Pink*. The comedic timing and romantic tension in this movie between the leads Molly Ringwald and Andrew McCarthy always gave me a honeyed feeling. But then you added Jon Cryer's unrequited love into the mix and the similarities to my situation kicked in. Not too long ago, I'd lived in a love triangle between Thorn, Erica, and myself.

My face warmed and I focused on the movie. How did you laugh and joke about a love triangle when you were in one with the person sitting across from you?

Even when Andie gently let down the delightfully quirky Duckie to be with the man of her dreams at prom, I kept my gaze laser-focused on the screen, hoping Erica didn't look at me. During the dance at the end of the movie, Andie chose Blane, leaving poor Duckie behind. Thorn hadn't refused Erica love privately. He'd chosen me over her in front of the entire pack.

The ultimate humiliation.

Maybe I should suggest a less touchy movie if we watched another one?

The credits rolled, and I should've smiled thinking of Blane and Andie's happily ever after, but I couldn't help stealing a glance at Erica. To my surprise, she had a blissful smile on her face. She even hugged one of the sofa pillows to her chest and grinned at Aggie.

"I could watch that movie over and over again," she purred. "I do wish Andie would've chosen Duckie, but I can understand why she fell in love with Blane."

"I still believe breakfast is better than boys," Aggie replied with a snort, "but I'd fall for Blane, too."

"He's everything and more," Erica agreed. "What do you think, Nat?"

Her genuine question made me smile. "What girl doesn't want a happily ever after?"

Next, Aggie popped in *Fight Club*, and I laughed. At least I wouldn't have to worry about this one.

"No more romance?" I asked.

"A girl ends up with a dude with a multiple personality disorder," Aggie explained. "Sounds like a romance to me."

I laughed. "I don't know if I'd want to hook up with a man who started a revolution and made soap from medical waste."

"I agree with Nat," Erica said. "That's really nasty."

Aggie stuck her tongue at us as we cackled. It was nice to be like this. If Erica had raised the white flag of surrender, maybe I needed to think about using mine too.

CHAPTER 13

After my fruitless search for the whistle yesterday, I couldn't help but feel frustrated. If Lady Ophelia had kept it safe in her hotel room instead of strolling around Central Park with it, we wouldn't have to deal with the leprechauns in the first place.

At least I hadn't left Seamus's shop empty-handed. Now I had a potential gift for Farley.

And to start my Sunday morning off right, I woke up to a silent house. Perhaps Farley had had a late movie marathon of Henry Fonda westerns, or he'd decided to get a good night's sleep for once. I finally had time to contemplate the missing whistle and the creatures that killed the night guard.

Long before I woke up, Nick had shot me a text with a kind offer to search again today, but I declined. Having that poor wizard follow me around didn't feel like a good use of his spare time. I wanted him to visit the clinic more often.

I'll text you every day until you send me a selfie of you in front of the clinic, I'd replied to him. *If you don't send me a pic in a day or two, we might need to take another field trip again.*

My reply came quickly. *That's fine.*

A win for the wolf, I say.

After dealing with Nick, I needed to figure out how to give Farley his gift. A part of me wanted to go all out and wrap up the damn thing using my egregious stash of holiday-oriented wrapping paper, but a man like him would probably mock my efforts.

I sighed. Why should I make all these plans when he might not care? I shoved my darkening mood aside and decided to get dressed. I had a world of garage sales to conquer, and on a gorgeous Sunday like today, plenty of them called my name. At every house, the owners would greet me with a grin, their tables and shelves filled with unwanted goodies. I'd gratefully rescue their grandmother's glass ornaments from the sixties, snag a perfect pair of baby overalls (for little Sveta), and I even tucked away a beautiful Christmas red KitchenAid mixer. And it didn't matter that I already had one.

Someday I might need to use both, right?

Once I gave in to my shopping urges and visited all the garage sales in the area, I surrendered to my next fix: to check in at The Bends to see what messes the staff had left me to clean up.

Only two hours had passed since the thrift store opened, but The Bends' parking lot, nestled between my workplace and another flea market, was full. Which meant I'd have plenty to do. From the lot, I walked past an outdoor shopping area filled with rows of tables. Everything appeared fine, other than stock tossed about, but I'd deal with that later. I headed inside to find customers, both human and supernatural of all shapes and sizes, browsing throughout the store. Instead of checking on them, I made a beeline for the double doors leading to the back office.

As I'd hoped, I spotted a tall, thin man with wire-framed

glasses sitting behind one of the work desks. He had a pile of pending invoices right in front of him, but he probably hadn't processed a single one. My goblin boss Bill might own the place, but I did most of the heavy lifting. Thanks to his enchantments, I could see through my customers' glamours and not fall for their simple attempts to mess with my head. Unfortunately, I could see through a weaker goblin's glamour, and I'd glimpsed Bill's true form. And he wasn't pretty. Nowadays, my boss strengthened his masking spell, and I appreciated the gesture.

"What are you doing here?" He pushed his glasses up. "Couldn't get enough of selling?" He flashed a smile. "I won't hold you back, but if you want to work here and at the demon's mart, I'm not paying you."

My smile died. Of course he wouldn't.

I told him what went down at Mademoiselle Midnight's, from the deadly creatures that lurked in town to, finally, my time in Brooklyn searching for the missing whistle.

"Damn, that sucks." He appeared thoughtful. "I wondered why The Bends keeps acting jittery at night."

"Have you, or the building itself, seen anything weird around here?"

"You mean other than Mrs. Kite's new girdle? That harpy keeps trying to stuff her birdie backside into that thing, and it isn't working."

I rolled my eyes. "I'm searching for two perpetrators. After I trailed after them that night, one of them burned me somehow. If that threat is still out there, I need to know what I'm facing."

"I haven't seen anything," Bill admitted. "But something is out there."

I sighed then snatched up the stack of invoices and sat at the opposite desk. Might as well relieve a little stress doing what I did best: keeping this place from going under.

I was halfway through the stack when I turned to see Bill standing beside me.

Did I do something wrong?

"You do plan to go back, don't you?" He sucked in a deep breath. "I have an agreement with Kramkar and the demons, and I'd rather not back out on it."

Was Bill fearful for once?

"I can't go back until I find the whistle," I said. "The night demon told me she'd filet me five ways from Sunday."

He nodded, and I paused my work to peer harder at him. Did that sneaky goblin know more about those demons?

"What do you know about Mademoiselle Midnight?" I asked. "If the pack has to make a final stand against her, I want to know any detail that might help."

He shrugged and stuffed his hands into his pockets. "There're some things even a goblin doesn't fuck with, and demons are one of them. If I was ever trapped, I'd gnaw my leg and arm off to get away. Ever since the Dark Ages, I've only run into a handful of them. They're a secretive lot, dealing with old elemental magic." His gaze fixed on the opposite side of the room as if he remembered the past. "Now that I think about it, right outside of Düsseldorf, I discovered Mimi and Dayla's little shop. Those ladies are quite the peculiar pair."

Wow, how old were they?

Bill continued. "I only saw Dayla during the daytime, while Mademoiselle Midnight moved about at night. While they sold their wares, they fed."

"Fed on what?"

He rolled his eyes. "Off the sun. Or the moon. Deep mystical shit like that. I just know light and dark are involved, but they also must feed off each other, as they grow weaker when they sleep. There's more to it than that, but that's too deep of a conversation for someone simple like me."

I recalled how Mimi mentioned she'd constructed her night guard from "night things." Did that mean she drew strength from the night to manipulate matter? And how could I use this information to defend the pack? I had no idea, but if one demon had to feed the other, they potentially had a weak point. As to how I'd exploit it if the moment arose, I didn't want to find out.

"I know that look," Bill said sternly. "You're thinking too much. You need to do your job and leave them alone. Demons are a dangerous lot." He scratched the top of his head. "The werewolves never have talked about it, but before you were born, demons rolled through here."

Now that caught my attention. "What happened?"

"Strange things went down. Crime went up. A missing kid or two sparked a lot of fear. Farley was a newly minted pack leader back then. At first, he approached the other supernaturals—me included. Usually, he respected us and let us do business as long as we didn't screw over the locals."

Bill got quiet. I'd never heard him speak like this. "When he figured out a bunch of demons were behind the crime in the area, I heard he met them and brokered a deal."

"What kind of deal?"

"I don't know, but I'd say he was clever. He didn't even need the pack, either. The next morning, the demons left, and he still had both arms and legs. Not long after that, he met Pearl and settled down a happy man."

After everything I'd gone through with Farley, it was good to hear he hadn't always been so bitter. Maybe someday I'd meet the brave leader who stood up to the demons and walked out alive to tell his tale.

CHAPTER 14

I wasn't sure if a miracle had occurred, but I returned to an empty house that afternoon. I could practically bathe in the ambiance. Not a single gunshot or horse stampede in sight. Glorious.

Thorn hadn't told me the Granthams had planned an outing, so I shot him a quick text: *Everything okay with Farley?*

Since I had the entire house to myself, I turned into a whirlwind and jumped from one cleaning task to another. While I vacuumed around the La-Z-Boy, yet again, I got a reply: *We're out shopping for supplies. Be back in a couple hours.*

The tension in my shoulders eased a bit. Thank goodness I didn't need to rush. I needed time to myself to find a happy medium, especially if this arrangement became a long-term deal. Suddenly, all the empty rooms at my old house came to mind. Not too long ago, I'd given the walls a fresh coat of paint and covered the furniture with cloths to keep the pests and dust mites at bay. Maybe if I broached the subject of Farley and Will staying there with Thorn, I couldn't walk away from the idea—no matter how badly Farley treated me.

I went about my chores, scrubbing down every surface

from the kitchen to the bathrooms. Eventually, I drifted to Farley's room, where I found all sorts of *treasures*. I counted three discarded shirts and a couple Fritos snack bags he'd snuck in here. He'd left both of the lamps in the room turned on, too. Farley had left the bed unmade—which I didn't mind. Why bother making it look nice when hours later you planned to sleep in it again? (I still made my bed, though.) While mumbling curses, I threw away the bunched-up tissues next to the bed.

Then I realized Farley hadn't complained about his chest cold lately.

Briefly, I stared at the small pile, and Farley's grief settled into me. Every day he lived in a room without family photos, his familiar bedspread, or the lingering scent of old cedar from the Grantham cabin. I had sparsely decorated this room with a vase, a couple of framed forest landscapes, and not much else. To him, this space was simply a hotel room.

How could I change that? The mementos from the cabin came to mind. I searched through the room, checking along the far wall until I spotted the plastic bin Will had carried inside. Farley had left a couple of Thorn's T-shirts on top of the box, so I missed it. Under normal circumstances, I would've ignored the container, but who couldn't look when the lid was slightly off?

I ambled over. What had Will rescued? At the top of the pile, I retrieved an 8x10 picture in a whiskey barrel wooden frame. The frame should've carried the scent of every person who touched it, but the fire had rubbed those memories away. I peered at a photo of the smiling Grantham family right outside of their cabin. An eight- or ten-year-old Thorn waved at the camera while a younger Farley rested on a canary-yellow lawn chair. Young Will stood there grinning as smoke rose off a nearby grill. What made me stare longer was the beaming woman sitting next to Farley. It was

Thorn's mother, Pearl. How beautiful she was. I could see Thorn's heartfelt smile in hers. She had an angelic, yet mesmerizing shine to her brown eyes. Pearl held a thick paperback near her face, but she must've paused to smile at the camera.

"Nice to see you again, Pearl," I said softly.

Underneath the first photos, I discovered many more. One featured an infant-age Thorn resting his head against his mother's chest while she cradled him close. Just looking at her photo reminded me of the few times I saw her at pack gatherings, since we'd never spoken to each other, and I regretted that. At least I had memories of her. She had a soft laugh and often hummed a little song while she fussed over her boys. Pearl Grantham even played cards with my uncles and won a hand or two. My heart hurt to see Farley smiling. He'd sat with the Stravinskys and broken bread with us.

Which meant the Farley I saw today wasn't the same man from back then.

I sighed. Time to put these photos where they belonged: out where we could admire them. First things first, I had to tackle the damage from the fire. Smoke and soot tended to stain and discolor photos. The sooner I cleaned them, the better. I fetched a bucket with my cotton cloth, glass cleaner, and oil soap. As I worked, I hoped Pearl would appreciate the care I used to remove the smudges and smears from every crack and crease. Broken frames got a staple or two to reinforce the weak points. Once I was pleased with my restoration handiwork, I arranged the photos on the dresser and the end table next to the bed.

"You have a beautiful family, Pearl," I said.

There were a few items left in the bin, so I organized those too. Might as well do what I could before Farley returned. At the bottom, I discovered a cigar box with a single photo tucked inside. I smiled at the picture of Pearl sitting in the cabin living room in front of their fireplace. On the mantel behind her, I spied a row of beautifully carved wolf figurines. As an antiquarian, I'd sold many a carving, but I'd never seen these before. The carver had meticulously crafted pieces with expressive eyes, pert ears, and thick tails. Had Pearl carved these herself, or had Farley made them? Maybe they'd purchased them somewhere?

I used my cell to take a picture of the photo and returned the keepsake to its original hiding place. As I left the room, I considered the gun I planned to wrap tonight. Would he accept it with an open heart, or did I need to find something else? Another idea came to mind, and I couldn't contain my excitement. Would Farley like one of these figurines if I found the manufacturer?

~

After cleaning the house, I had little energy for much else, but a predator potentially lurked around town. And that meant I had to participate in pack patrols.

"What time is everyone meeting up?" I asked Thorn while I prepared spicy enchiladas for dinner. After Thorn and his family returned with their purchases, my mate and I had gathered in the kitchen to figure out our plans for the evening.

"Everyone needs a break." He shook his head. "I don't want to think about the whistle or that thing—"

"But what if someone buys it?" I asked. "In a place like New York, what can go wrong will go wrong."

His face reflected the confidence I needed. "Then we'll face the consequences together."

I still itched to search for the whistle tonight. "What if we had a date night in the city?"

That got a grin out of him. "And I'm sure this date night includes visiting pawn shops?"

"Not necessarily, but if we ate at this one Italian spot in Queens, we could hit four pawn shops nearby. They've got this ah-mazing chestnut tortelli dish."

"Uh-huh."

"A garlic-and-chile-suffused angel-hair pasta worth shaving your head to eat."

Thorn laughed and drew me into his arms. I rested my cheek against his heart. Feeling his steady heartbeat thrum against my face sounded better than any jazz music I'd ever heard.

"So, I can't entice you with their world-renowned lasagna made by the owner's grandma from Sicily?" I whispered.

"I'm sure it's amazing, but we could save some gas and stay home," he murmured against my head. "I could hunt for that ticklish spot on your inner thigh—"

The TV volume in the living room abruptly rose.

"Could you at least do that after I go to sleep?" Will called out from the living room.

"Should I shout it out, then?" Thorn replied. Werewolf hearing in this house made privacy a moot point.

"Hell no," Will said.

Thorn kissed my neck, eliciting a squeal from me.

"I need to find us a place to live, Dad," Will said.

Thorn's smirk and darkened hazel eyes promised he wouldn't behave tonight. I ran my hands down his back, tracing my fingers along his hard muscles. Having his body pressed against mine left me urgent with need. In particular, a need for him to take me into the bedroom and make me forget about the whistle, demons, and anything else that plagued our town. Thorn kissed me again, and I couldn't hold back my pleased hum. I would've gladly forgotten the dish of enchiladas I was preparing if we hadn't heard a hard knock on the front door. Thorn's head rose.

"I'll get it." The heavy footfalls of Will's footsteps reached the front door.

Moments later, I was surprised to see Rex striding into the kitchen. The concerned expression on his face drew Thorn and I apart.

"Something's wrong, isn't it?" I asked Rex.

"We found a body at the butcher shop," Rex said. "It was one of us this time."

CHAPTER 15

Somber pack members congregated outside of Dalton's Meats off Double Trouble Road. The men and women's morose expressions and lowered shoulders didn't lift as Thorn, Will, Farley, and I showed up.

I spotted my dad among them, and my stomach sank. That wasn't a good sign.

For a private pack matter like this, no one called the police or an ambulance—which meant we'd settle the matter in-house, too.

With a sigh, I took in the meat market I'd entered countless times as a kid. Frank Dalton owned the place and delivered anything my family needed. Most of the grocery stores in town sold meat, but if you wanted larger portions, you bought your slabs from Frank and his two daughters. I swallowed deeply, not wanting to know yet who'd died. I grew up with Bella and Francine. Those girls had loved ones, too.

I respectfully nodded to my father and the other pack members. Farley was the last of us to join the group. He limped up with a growing frown.

"Evening, Farley," Dad called out to him.

"I wish I could say it was a good evening, Fyodor," Farley replied quietly.

Everyone turned toward the butcher shop. Might as well get down to business.

"Who died?" Thorn asked gently.

"It was Francine." Dad stared down at his clasped hands. "When she didn't come home from work, her husband called Frank to check the shop." He gestured for us to follow him inside. Within two steps I caught the telltale hints of death hidden underneath the coppery scent of butchered meat.

My heart clenched.

All this trouble had occurred as Francine closed up the storefront. Cuts of meat were still arranged in the refrigerated display, and the OPEN sign flashed on and off.

"This wasn't a robbery," I said.

"Yeah, the piece of trash who did this didn't want money," Farley said stiffly.

Thorn looked to Will, then the older brother glanced at the sign. With an unspoken word between brothers, Will turned off the OPEN sign.

"Where's Frank?" Thorn asked. "No one left him alone, did they?"

"Rex took him out for a drive," Dad explained. "Frank wanted to hunt for his daughter's killer, so it was best for him not to stay here."

Dread soured my stomach as we marched around the meat display counter to an open door that led to the back office and freezer. Cool air from the freezer fanned my face.

Slowly, we entered single file into the chilled room. The well-lit space was organized with pork and beef slabs hung from hooks in one corner, while in another corner the Dalton family had set up a counter to package and seal their products.

What was left of poor Francine Dalton lay sprawled in

the middle of the room. The dark-haired woman's neck was bent at an odd angle and her vacant gray eyes stared upward. Her attacker had slashed her open, spreading blood across the cement floor. Paw prints peppered the floor around her.

I bit my lower lip to keep myself from cursing.

"What did this?" Thorn asked bitterly.

"An animal that's strong like us, with large claws and teeth," Dad replied.

I wanted to look away, but I forced myself to take note of any information I could use to find Francine's killer. In particular, I spotted bloody prints on the floor. They led to the open door to the loading dock.

"There are bloody paw prints only around the body, and their path heads out the door," I said. "I didn't see any in the front."

"Which means the fight took place here," Farley said with a nod. "She discovered her attackers, and they took her down somehow."

Dad's sharp eyes swept over the room. "See how Francine's neck is snapped. There's no bite marks—which means the biped creature we're searching for helped the animal subdue her."

"What kind of hit would break a wolf's neck?" Will asked.

The heavy clang of a weapon hitting the goblin shield reverberated through me. "The hit came from the blunt end of a weapon, and the wielder was very strong," I murmured. "I'm certain only a shield could withstand that kind of hit."

The goblin shield did reveal a clue I hadn't thought about until now: the spikes were on fire.

"Whatever it is," I added, "it's susceptible to fire. Mademoiselle Midnight said someone stole another artifact to protect it from heat."

"We need to find them," Thorn said bitterly.

"Yes, we do, but how?" I asked.

That question circled the room, but no one had any answers.

Will finally spoke up. "What I want to know is: why did they come *here?*"

Good question.

"Look at those slabs of beef, boy." Farley pointed. "I bet my shitty knee they came to feed the animal."

At first, I thought Frank had sheared the meat off the slabs, but as Farley mentioned, hunks were torn off. So not only did we have murderers on our hands, but one of them needed to eat raw meat. As much as I'd hoped my attackers returned to New York to fight Lisbetta, I wanted them to stick around so we could hunt them down.

No one said a word as Thorn and Will draped a tarp over Francine. Dad murmured a prayer for her safe passage while Farley fumed.

"Not a single drop of their blood on the floor," Thorn's father grumbled, his voice rising with anger. "What a waste of a good woman. She was a strong girl…better than most." Briefly, he glared at me, and I turned away. No one caught the jab he'd made at me, and as much as I wanted to call him out, now wasn't the time for us to butt heads.

"What do we do now?" Will asked.

All eyes turned to Thorn.

"We fight back." Thorn's hardened gaze never left the tarp. "This is our territory. If they want to face the pack's fury, we'll oblige them."

We didn't return home until long after midnight. Thorn and I waited with Francine's family to make the final arrangements. Pack members connected with the local police department would handle her disappearance.

From now on, the pack would whisper Francine's name with reverence and pain.

We'd also have to bury her later this week.

The idea Francine died, that someone I saw a couple times a week when I shopped there was gone, knocked me off-kilter. The pack hunted and battled together. Sometimes our brothers and sisters didn't make it home, but those deaths were few and far between.

The silent car ride home led to a silent household. Will collapsed onto the couch while Farley slipped into his room and shut the door.

Thorn and I took our time, going through the motions of securing the house and turning off the lights. As we settled into bed, I should've fallen asleep immediately, but I couldn't shake the flash of resentment in Farley's eyes.

"What a waste of a good woman," he'd said. "She was a strong girl…better than most."

Would he have said those same words if I'd passed away? I didn't believe so, based on our history.

I rested my head against Thorn's shoulder and held him tight. The world should've righted itself as we rested chest to chest and heart to heart in our bed, but I was cast adrift again.

"You okay?" he murmured against my forehead. "Everything's fucked up right now, but we'll get through this together."

"It's more than the mess outside." I pointed to my heart. "It's this that hurts."

I drew a deep breath before I spoke again. "Do you remember the night Farley wanted me to leave South Toms River for good? It was not long after the Long Island werewolves threatened to take over."

Thorn nodded. "I remember."

"I felt incredibly lost that night." My voice grew thick, but

I forced myself to keep going. "I *need* to be strong right now, but I can't help but feel useless."

Thorn stilled. "Has my father said anything to you recently? If he's crossed the line, I'll take him to a motel. I mean it, babe."

I shook my head. "Kicking him out of the house won't solve the problem," I whispered. "He'll always be the former pack leader and your father. His words will always carry weight."

"His words carry weight if you *let* them," Thorn said. "The past will always be there. You should focus on this moment. Right here. Right now."

As hard as I tried to settle into the warmth of the here and now, the weight of Farley's words remained. Thorn cradled my face in his large hand to offer comfort, but I couldn't escape falling into the memories of that horrible night. I tried to conjure spry jackrabbits and juicy squirrels giving me chase, but the cabin's great room and Farley's dominating presence crept in. I was back in that room with Farley in his chair and me perched on his couch.

The words he'd said that night bounced off the walls.

"I told you the weakest link brings down the pack," Farley had said. "But you didn't listen. Not surprised, though. You're like your grandmother in that regard. I can see you don't hold the pack's safety before your own."

I wanted to wake up, but the dream had me in its icy grip. I had to witness Farley's rejection again.

"Since you are a liability to the safety of the pack," he said firmly, "I have no choice but to force you to leave our territory."

The former pack leader didn't blink as he added, "If the Long Island and Burlington werewolf packs are not driven off within that time, you must leave—or the pack will mark you for execution." His gaze burrowed into mine. It was a split second too long before I glanced down. "I will *execute* you myself if necessary."

A cold sweat formed on my brow from the memory as I returned to the present and shivered in my bed.

Less than a year ago, my father-in-law was willing to kill me for the *good* of the pack.

He was willing to cast me out to keep me away from his son.

But like Thorn told me, the past was the past. The world had changed for the better since that night. The pack drove our rivals away, but Farley and I had never addressed his feelings for me. All this time, he still believed I wasn't good enough for the pack or his son.

"I'm not stupid, girl," he'd also said that night. "I can see the way my boy looks at you. You're more than a liability to the pack. You're a liability to *him* as well." He snorted out the word *him*. "I can't believe he tried to defend you. Defend what you *are*. A bunch of words about what you've done in the past won't help us now. We're vulnerable, and we don't need your *kind* around here."

As Thorn held me like he'd never let me go, I considered the kind of woman I'd become since that night. How I'd stood up and fought when others retreated. How I'd sacrificed myself while others hid away.

But Farley and I still had work to do. One of us had to step over the gulf and build the bridge. As much as I didn't want to remember the pain or put in the work, I knew in my heart it was the right thing to do for both of us.

CHAPTER 16

Today, I woke up refreshed and ready to act instead of reacting. I'd licked my wounds, and now I had work to do. As the pack's alpha female, I had to reach out to the Dalton family and volunteer to help with any final preparations. Other pack members might need emotional support, too.

From the privacy of my bedroom, I made the phone calls in a thankfully quiet home. After I reached out to Francine's husband, I plodded out to the kitchen to find Farley nursing a cup of black coffee at the kitchen table.

The present I'd boxed up with a bright red ribbon sat on the counter on top of my Christmas cookbooks. I'd paid a pretty penny for that thing. Did he even deserve it after what happened last night?

I went through the motions of preparing a cup of tea, unsure what to say. As much as I wanted to escape the house, I was determined to see things through. Dr. Frank had given me this assignment for a reason.

Build a bridge over the gulf, Nat.

"You hungry?" I finally asked.

Step one achieved: civility.

He slowly shook his head. We didn't speak for a couple of minutes, and I wondered if he didn't want to talk to me.

Then, out of nowhere, Farley broke the silence. "Damn shame what happened to Francine Dalton."

"Yes, it is." I waited for him to add more about me.

"Whatever killed her will kill again."

I nodded. We at least agreed on that.

"Has Thorn warned the pack to keep an eye on the pups?" he asked.

"Yes, all children must go directly home from school, and any pack-owned stores are on alert."

His wrinkled face grew pensive. "That's good."

He took a sip of his coffee. Steam no longer rose from the cup. How could he drink it cold?

I forced myself to use the moment to pick up his cup. He protested until he noticed I placed the cup in the microwave. Twenty seconds later, I delivered his hot coffee and the present.

"What's this?" he grunted.

"A gift."

"I can see that. Why?"

Damn, I hadn't prepared myself for that question. "You lost your house, so I thought it would be nice for you to have something new."

Farley stared at the box for a bit.

"It's not a glitter bomb," I added dryly.

Reluctantly, he untied the ribbon and removed the top. Carefully, he withdrew the Colt Navy Revolver. I held my breath for his reaction.

Not a single muscle twitched on his face. No frown. No grimace. Not even a half-assed smile.

"What am I supposed to do with this?" he said. "You remember the Code, don't you?"

I tried to smile, and my face broke. Most folks at least tried to say thanks first. "Yes, werewolves shouldn't own or use firearms, but this is a *collector's* piece." My voice picked up as I gave the weapon's background. "We could have it arranged in a custom frame at your new house."

Farley's Adam's apple bobbed a couple of times, but his face showed indifference. He palmed the gun, turning it over twice, but didn't show genuine interest. "Looks nice."

My gesture had crashed and burned.

Well, that hurt, but then again, bridges weren't built in a day.

"Thanks," he added, then put the gun back into the box.

An awkward silence swept into the kitchen, and I stood there trying to keep my frustration at bay.

Step two: maintain the civility.

To distract myself, I started wiping off the counter—which was already clean, mind you. In the middle of mopping the floors, I was surprised to hear Farley address me from the other side of the room.

"I need to borrow your car this morning," he mumbled. "Is that possible?"

He could've demanded to use it, but the request made me pause. "Sure. Do you need me to pick up something for you, so you don't have to walk far?"

Farley shook his head as his stomach growled. So, he hadn't eaten. "I need to go pay my respects to the Daltons. Maybe I'll check out a few apartments, too."

"Not a problem. I planned to work this morning, anyway. I can take you wherever you need to go, but you should eat first." I opened the fridge and fetched the ingredients to make waffles.

I almost dropped the carton of eggs when Farley gruffly said, "Sounds good. Thanks."

My gaze jumped from the gift to the man sitting at the table.

Step three: never give up the good fight.

Farley hadn't accepted my gift with an open heart, but something else happened this morning. I hid a smile and whistled while I started cooking.

~

I nstead of taking my father-in-law to Francine Dalton's home, Farley dropped me off at The Bends. I hadn't seen him drive in a long time. Hopefully, the car helped him today.

It wasn't like I had any elaborate plans. I could escape to the city and search, but I couldn't do it alone, so I came here to scratch an itch. The Bends served as the perfect distraction. Normal people would've stayed home and slept in, but I marched into the thrift store ready to lose myself in furniture polish, irate customers, and a stubborn boss.

I'd picked the perfect morning, too. A tour bus full of senior shoppers pulled into the parking lot. Inside the store, a minotaur couple, two brownies, and Valkyrie browsed. Not long after I entered, the human deluge followed. The humans chirped, gawked, and admired our Victorian furniture while the minotaur couple ambled up to the registers to purchase an enchanted collection of brass bull nose rings.

This chaos is better than therapy, I thought.

I took my time to tidy the fallen magical capes the brownies rifled through and line up the Haunted Heather figurines. Right on cue, the porcelain figures moaned when I shifted them to the right place.

All was almost right with the world until I noticed a large line forming for the checkout. Naturally, Bill was nowhere to be found, and I'd yet to see him manning the registers during the larger summer crowds.

I searched for our fastest cashier, and the fire witch had disappeared too. Probably lighting up another cigarette on the loading dock. At least she hadn't set fire to the place while I was away. I abandoned my current task and jumped into the fray. How I missed this part. I reveled in the delightful clicking sounds of the keys on the registers. The *beepity beeps* from the credit card machines as sales went through. Those noises sounded just as good as the times when I bought something.

Once I got the line down to a single man trying to purchase an antique kite from the 1860s, I escaped to the back office for a drink. Of course, I found good ole Bill with his feet propped up and his eyes on his cell phone.

I had a seat at a computer station and checked my text messages. Aggie had sent me two funny YouTube videos. And I'd gotten a message from Farley, too: *Thorn will pick you up tonight.*

I reread the message and checked to see if I'd mistaken the sender. Nope, he'd really sent me a message.

I tried not to think about why he needed my car all day, but then again, if Farley planned to check out a couple of apartments, he'd need it. And, well, he didn't seem like the type to go drag racing and such.

I tried to dive back into cataloguing new products, but after Farley's text, I couldn't stop thinking about what happened this morning. The gift hadn't gone over well, but I was determined to try again. Briefly, I picked up my phone to find the picture I'd taken of the figurine from the Grantham cabin. With that image in hand, I scoured the Internet and the catalogues we owned, but I didn't find anything. Did that mean it was homemade?

Bill appeared to be doing a lot of nothing, so I

approached him. "Hey, Bill, I'm trying to find information on a carving. Got a moment to take a look?"

"Nope." He put down his phone and put his hands behind his head.

"Since I'm working for free today, would it hurt for you to give your professional opinion? You do have *centuries* of experience." I emphasized the word *centuries* with flourish.

He slowly nodded. "You have a point there. Whatcha got?"

I showed him the picture of Pearl with the figurines.

"Hmmm." He turned the phone this way and that. Zoomed in and out.

"Anything?"

"You can't buy those anywhere." He added softly, "Long time no see, Pearl."

My mouth parted. Had Bill met her before? "What do you mean I can't *buy* them? Does that mean they're not made anymore?"

"Those didn't come from a factory. They were made by hand."

When I gave him a questioning look, he stared back at me with time-to-teach-the-amateur expression. "Back in the Dark Ages, folks didn't make that cheap shit you see nowadays. Rich merchants paid a pretty pound to people like me for the fake stuff, but there were dirt-poor craftsmen out there who could make works of art like those."

He stared a bit harder at the image. "The original crafter didn't use a carving knife, either."

"Are you sure?"

He pursed his lips. "I'm very sure. Be quiet and listen. A long time ago, I met a werewolf who carved that kind of thing with his claws." He nodded. "Yup, a carver with claws made these."

Now that Bill had done his due diligence for the day and helped a newbie, he abandoned my phone and waltzed over to some crusty old donuts. To my disgust, he helped himself to one.

I switched my attention back to the photo, admiring the wooden art in a new light. A thought came to mind, but once I thought of it, I couldn't walk away from it: had Pearl made these? None of the pictures depicted her crafting them. Maybe it was Farley? The way she lovingly held one made my heart squeeze. It wasn't pride in her eyes, but love.

I held my breath as I considered the next step. Finding the right piece of wood wouldn't take long. I recognized the black walnut from the grain.

But what would Farley think of my gesture?

Every day he sat in that chair and lost himself while he watched shows. He had to miss Pearl. He wouldn't even let Thorn mention her name. Would giving him the wood to begin carving again open his wounds even further?

I considered that, and many other things, as I finished working a half-shift that day. When I was ready to leave, I shot a text to Thorn and decided to wait for him on the back dock. The moment I finished the text message, my phone rang with a call from an unknown NYC number. Tentatively, I accepted.

"Good afternoon, lass," came a voice with a strong Irish burr.

"Hello, Seamus, what an unexpected *pleasure*." Good God, what did the leprechaun want? And how did he get my number?

"After you came by the other day, I kept thinking about your quest to find that whistle."

"Did you now?"

"I reached out to my associates in the business, and one of them has what you're looking for."

If I had ears on the top of my head, they would've perked up. "Where is it?"

"Why, it's here with me now in my shop." I could imagine the smug look on his face. "I paid a pretty penny for it, too."

Here it comes. "And what pretty penny would *I* need to pay?"

"You'll have to come down to O'Malley's so we can discuss the matter."

I switched from resting on one leg to another. If I'd met one sleazeball, I'd met them all. "We can discuss this now. I happen to work long hours."

That got an audible sigh out of him. "I prefer face-to-face interaction, is all."

"Does that face-to-face interaction include the spell you tried to cast on me the other day?"

He chuckled. "Now, now, sweet lady. You can't hate a leprechaun for admiring a pretty girl. One as nice as you could make some coins instead of working out of that goblin's shack."

My breath caught. Had he followed me? "How do you know where I work?"

"These days I don't need magic when I got the Internet. There's not many Natalya Stravinskys out there, and when I discovered you worked at The Bend of the River Flea Market, I understood how you deftly negotiated the gun's price."

"Which means, from one antiquarian to another, I know you're going to try to hustle me if I want that whistle."

"A hustle? No, no. I want a fair price for my hard work."

"I don't have the money." And that was the truth, unfortunately.

"We could come to an arrangement, then—"

"I work a minimum-wage gig. I don't want to be one of your girls, and I'd tear your throat out if you ever laid a hand on me."

His boisterous laugh pissed me off even more. "You're a

feisty one. I like that. You're also smarter than most. Having an employee like you makes Bill one lucky goblin."

Oh, no. I could smell where this conversation was going. The leprechaun wanted to make a deal of some kind.

Seamus continued. "The way I see it, you're not interested in working in my *other* businesses, but I could use you as a buyer."

"I don't have experience as a buyer. Bill took care of that."

"That's a shame. There's a lot to learn. I could teach you those things…if you're interested in handling five deals for me in exchange for the whistle."

I bit my lower lip. After everything I'd been through with Kramkar, up to the night demon and her ceramic shop, an intelligent person would tell the leprechaun to go fuck himself, and hang up the phone, but I wasn't in that position.

If I didn't take the deal, he'd sell it and Mademoiselle Midnight would unleash her fury on the pack. Again and again, the supernatural world seemed to slam my back against the wall to where I was given a choice to cower or stand up and fight.

The South Toms River Pack is yours now, I reminded myself. Farley's words couldn't take that away from me.

"I'll agree to your terms based on the following conditions: I will not buy anything lewd or alive. Every purchase I make will use cash or a currency I can recognize. You cannot use me as barter for something else. If I cannot complete your tasks in one month, no deal."

I faintly heard him tapping something hard with his fingertips while he considered my constraints. "I can see working with the goblin has rubbed off on you, girl. I almost want to say no, but I'm curious to see what you can do for me and my business. You might be the opportunity I'm looking for."

"Then you'll give me the whistle tonight and we'll shake… err, verbally make our agreement?"

"Agreed." He chuckled and hung up.

For a second, I stood there. Then I sagged against The Bends. The gravity of what I'd done squeezed my head until my vision blurred and my chest tightened.

Someone shifted beside me. I spun to see Bill with folded arms and a harsh frown. "I don't know if you're about as smart as the talking abscess on my crooked left toe or you're a genius of your generation. My vote's for the former."

CHAPTER 17

That evening, I sat with the Grantham men in the living room and told them the somewhat good news: I'd discovered the whistle's location. Naturally, the Grantham men weren't thrilled I'd have to make a deal with a leprechaun to secure the whistle.

"Those fuckers need to stick to cereal and stop screwing around with people," Farley grumbled from the La-Z-Boy.

I'd give a million bucks if a box of Lucky Charms cereal was the root of our problems.

Thorn's lips were pressed into a white slash. "I don't trust Seamus. I'll get the whistle for you."

"My deal is with him," I said firmly. "We'll go together."

"I don't care who goes," Farley told us. "Just get the whistle and return the damn thing to that demon. I've had dealings with them in the past, and they're as trustworthy as a wobbly backup tire."

Will asked to help, but Thorn shot down his brother's plan. "Defend the den. We don't know if those two creatures are roaming town."

"Fine, but you get to have all the fun. I'm gonna check the property." Will stomped out of the house.

I swallowed a laugh. This shit wasn't fun.

With a plan in place, I changed out of my blouse and pencil skirt to jeans and running shoes. If something went down during the exchange tonight, I didn't want low heels to be the reason I got killed.

An hour later, we didn't venture into New York alone. Since I had to deal with a creature capable of using enchantments, we brought Brenna along for backup. While we drove into Manhattan, I updated her on what had happened so far.

After I finished, she said, "Geez, you can never get a break, can you?"

"It's the story of my life," I replied.

From the driver seat, Thorn added, "Speaking of breaks, weren't we supposed to plan a trip to Maine this summer?"

Ah yes, the Maine trip. I'd dreamt of finding a cozy cabin deep in the woods. I'd even started collecting fly-fishing lures so Thorn and I could immerse ourselves in nature. We'd fish during the day. Feel the forest breeze through the trees and hunt for small prey at night. We'd make out like bunnies whenever we wanted.

"I still want to reserve a cabin," I admitted. "We've never had a good time to leave."

"You might never leave at this rate," Brenna said.

Soon enough, we drove through Manhattan, then made our way to Queens. Finding a place to park would prove more difficult than facing the leprechaun.

While we hunted for a spot, I turned to Brenna. "I don't know much about leprechaun magic. Any details so we don't go in blind?"

Brenna released a subdued laugh. "If you thought your boss loved money, leprechauns got them beat. They're persistent and underhanded survivors, first and foremost. Always assume his intentions are related to profit."

"What kind of powers do they have?" Thorn asked.

"Their strength lies in persuasion, and it's all based on proximity. The closer you are to them, the more you're compelled to obey."

I frowned, recalling how Seamus tried to cast a spell on me. "Is there anything we can use to block the spell's effects?" I asked.

"Other that a counter-spell, your best bet is to get as far away from him as possible," she said softly.

Which meant I'd either had to make a run for it or use Old Magic. Since I'd never learned how to reflect magic, I'd have to tuck my tail between my legs and escape. Lovely.

After circling the neighborhood over ten times, we finally slipped into an open space when a man suddenly pulled away.

"Next time we need to use a jump point," Brenna said with a chuckle.

"We shouldn't use magic unless necessary," Thorn grumbled.

"You can't tell me this doesn't suck." Brenna shook her head. "I never drive into the city anymore unless I have no choice. I can't fit a car inside my enchanted pockets yet."

We had to park a mile away from the shop, but ten minutes later, we finally strolled up to O'Malley's Pawn and Jewelry. The store's interior was well lit. From the back of the store, Seamus waved to us. He wasn't alone this time. A couple of scantily clad ladies sat here and there.

Was this a pawn shop or a brothel?

One of girls, a pouty little brunette, briefly put down her *Cosmo* magazine to smile at us.

When we didn't return the gesture, she probably got back

to a top ten list of ways to make your lover fall in love with your inner goddess.

"Good to see you, Miss Stravinsky." Instead of checking me out, Seamus's eyeballs stroked Brenna up and down. "Happy to be doing business with you tonight."

"Where's the whistle?" I asked, getting to the point.

"Now, now," Seamus said. "You can't pay a visit and not introduce your friends."

"I want to know his name," a saucy redhead said, her gaze fixed on Thorn.

"I'm the *husband*," Thorn said darkly.

"No need for my name," Brenna added. "Not today. Not ever."

That got a frown from the leprechaun, but he switched back to business with a jerk of his ringed fingers. "Go bring me what they want, Lila."

The saucy redhead blew a kiss to Thorn, then disappeared into through the door behind the leprechaun. A minute later, she reappeared with a beat-up leather suitcase. Seamus fumbled with the locks, even glancing up to make sure we didn't peek. Then he opened the suitcase and turned it around to reveal the whistle nestled on a red velvet pillow.

"Is that it?" I asked Brenna. "No glamours?"

"I sense power around it," she replied, "but I'm not sure."

Damn it. "I know this wasn't a part of our deal, but can I touch it?"

The leprechaun grinned. "Nope."

That got a growl out of Thorn.

"Easy now, lad," Seamus said. "Neither of us trust each other. That won't change."

I recalled the night demon telling me I'd recognize the whistle if I was willing to search for it. Would Old Magic do the trick?

"Reaching out to find light in the darkness costs nothing,"

Mevelyn had told me. Maybe I could verify I'd found it by tapping into the power I used the night I broke into Kramkar's shop.

I closed my eyes and drew in a deep breath. Held it. I cradled everything that represented the outside within me. The magic returned in a rush, and even with my eyes closed, the magical essence of those around me burned bright like twinkling galaxies. The pawn shop had sprinkles of magical items here and there. A wand was hidden among toys, and a watch wound backward instead of forward.

The item in question flared the brightest of them all. The whistle sparkled with white flecks like opal. And right along the side, I spied a single tiny paw print.

I'd found it.

I glanced up to see Seamus's true form. Ugh, he wasn't pretty. He had tiny scars on his hands and teeth far too big for his mouth, and his slicked-back red hair was patchy in spots.

I blinked and released the breath I held to draw myself out of the spell. "That's it. We found it."

"Indeed, you have found it," the leprechaun said with gusto. "I've found quite the handy wolf to work with in the future."

Thorn appeared none too pleased with that remark and advanced on the leprechaun.

I raised my hand. "He's not really there."

"Your wife's right, laddie," Seamus said. "Calm yourself and let's finish our deal."

"Then how does she get the whistle?" Thorn asked.

"After we make our deal." The leprechaun turned to me. "Do we have a deal?"

I repeated the terms from memory, but I added one more detail: no work until I dealt with the demons, then I could complete the five purchases.

"Fair enough," he added. "I want your full attention."

"Then we have a deal, Seamus."

The whistle vanished from the suitcase and appeared on the counter. I snatched my prize before he could change his mind.

Seamus's grin spread wide enough to reveal a golden molar. "It was a pleasure doing business with you, lass. I look forward to seeing your lovely backside as you leave."

We quickly left the store to the warm evening outside.

"Are you sure I can't hurt him?" Thorn growled.

"Even I can shove some bushes up his ass," Brenna offered.

"Don't tempt me," I replied.

We walked down the street, and I couldn't believe I held the whistle in my hand. I felt like I carried the weight of the world in my palm. It was amazing how such a simple thing could summon a powerful beast to do my bidding. I could drive away the two predators that roamed South Toms River, or even a goddess.

"What's up, Nat?" Brenna asked.

I glanced up to see I'd stopped in the middle of the street. I hurried to catch up with them. "I was thinking."

"Not sure if that's a good thing or bad thing right now," Thorn said.

"All the trouble we've had with She Who Always Walks the Path could end the moment I summon Cerberus." After that, we wouldn't deal with predators or opportunists coming into town to cheat the population and leave us scrambling.

Brenna scoffed. "Yes, it would, but after everything you've learned, do you want to take that chance? What if Cerberus shows up in the middle of Fifth Avenue?"

"And what happens after Cerberus drives the goddess

away?" Thorn added. "Can you guarantee you'll have absolute control over the hellhound?"

I sighed and gripped the warm ceramic pipe. The whistle promised a song that would finally sever the tie between the goddess and myself.

Brenna extended her hand to me. "Do you need me to hold it for you until we get home?"

I swallowed past the massive lump in my throat. "No, I'm good."

"I know you're tempted, but we have more questions than answers." Brenna appeared to consider what she said before she spoke. "If you want, I can ask the Witches' Guild if they have any advice on the matter."

"Would they come take it from us?" Thorn asked.

"I won't reveal any details," Brenna replied. "Rest assured."

Thorn and I agreed to those terms. A day or two, at the most, would give the Witches' Guild time to dig for any information. After that, I wouldn't have any regrets when I returned the whistle to the demons.

As we headed to the car, I should've felt reassured, but doubts circled my head and remained to dig into my skin.

CHAPTER 18

Not long into our drive back to Jersey, I got a text message from my mom inviting the Granthams over for dinner at their house. As weary as I felt after working today and facing Seamus, the very idea of diving face-first into a Stravinsky family meal relaxed me a little.

There was nothing like home cooking and my family's antics to make a day end well.

I told Thorn, and he chuckled.

"What's wrong?" I asked.

"Did they mean *all* the Granthams, or just Will and me?"

"Knowing my family, they want everyone to come over so they can make sure Farley is behaving."

"Good point. So how do we make him go? He's never gone before."

True, but like all werewolves, Farley often thought with his stomach.

I asked Brenna if she wanted dinner, but she declined. "Nick invited me over."

"You should definitely skip my family dinner, then." I returned her smile and thanked her for her help.

After we dropped off Brenna at her apartment, we returned home to find Farley fast asleep in front of the television. His mouth hung wide open as he maintained a tight grip around a beer.

He wasn't alone, either.

Thorn and I paused at the edge of the living room and gaped.

Our intruder, which stood no taller than my knee, perched on the sofa next to Farley and helped itself to the beer nuts in the bowl on the coffee table. The red and white cotton clothes it wore were threadbare, but its silver buckle shoes shone. Its wrinkled face scrunched up as it gobbled up the goods.

"What is it?" Thorn mumbled. My mate's body tensed as he prepared to pounce on the intruder, but I grabbed his shoulder when the creature leaned forward and wrested the beer from Farley's hand—without waking the wolf up.

"I think that's a clurichaun," I whispered.

"What is that?" Thorn took a step into the living room.

The clurichaun guzzled down the beer, smirked at us, then tossed the bottle at Thorn's head. With an annoyed growl, my mate caught the bottle in midair. The creature used the diversion to make a run for it into the kitchen.

We darted after it, but our visitor escaped out the back door and into the night.

Thorn circled the house, but I doubted he'd find it.

My mate returned inside, all the while shaking his head with a grin. "It's gone."

"It's probably in the cellar," I explained. "Back when the Basilisk King started to leave chests everywhere, Karey and the other wood nymphs searched the house. She told me the place was safe, but that we had one of those things sleeping in the cellar."

"Is it dangerous?"

"Not really. Karey told me they're drunken troublemakers."

That got an amused snort out of Thorn, and I couldn't help but laugh with him. Some folks dealt with bats in the attic or bugs behind the fridge. We had a drunken fairy in the cellar, but at least it hadn't harmed anyone.

"Do you think it will come back?" Thorn added.

"Probably. Have you seen how much alcohol we've had in the house lately?"

Thorn peeked into the fridge and sighed at seeing how many bottles of beer we had left. "I'll take these out to the SUV. We can leave them over at your parents' house."

The moment Thorn had stowed the bottles away in a box, Farley woke up to start a fuss. "What are you doing with my beer, boy?" he snapped.

"We got a pest problem." Thorn explained the issue with the fairy in the cellar.

Farley harrumphed. "Can't we set some traps? Maybe kill it with bug spray?"

I gave a quick smile at the thought of taking the clurichaun down like a cockroach. "How about we leave it alone for now?"

That got me a scowl from Farley, but I ignored him to say, "Look, my parents invited us over for dinner. You could hang out and have some cold beers with my family."

Farley scratched at his shaggy blond hair. His scowl deepened as if he considered refusing our offer, but eventually he nodded.

With that matter settled, I considered hiding the whistle in the house, but since no one would be home to guard it, I nestled the whistle into my pants pocket for safekeeping.

Ten minutes later, we parked behind a bunch of cars next to my parents' Colonial-style home. I'd expected a small family dinner, but as usual, the Stravinskys had decided to invite every werewolf in town. A few pack members arrived before us, and I could hear their raucous laughter from outside the house.

I glanced at my father-in-law in the back seat. He clung to the box of beer like he didn't want to share it. Since he knew the Stravinskys well, that might be the best plan of action.

After Thorn and I left the SUV, Farley reluctantly got out and limped up after us. I opened the front door and the noise rolled over us, but I embraced it. We'd arrived just in time, too. I caught the decadent scent of chicken *tabaka*. As a child I loved to watch Mom prep the chickens, sprinkle them with seasonings like cilantro, turmeric, and garlic, then fry them until the skin turned brown and crispy. My mouth watered as I imagined the meat settled in oil and sizzling in the cast-iron skillet.

There's no better place than home base, I thought.

I'd yet to see Mom ruin a dish—unless Dad distracted her. And I suspected after he did the deed, he'd disappear for a couple of days to escape her wrath.

Members of the Stravinsky clan, as well as a pocket of pack members, had stuffed themselves throughout the living room, kitchen, and dining room. Kids darted from one of the bedrooms and squeezed around us to go play outside. I didn't want to sit anyway when Mom would have a plate ready and waiting.

Thorn nudged his dad into the room. On the TV, the cheers from a recorded soccer match in Russia were nothing compared to the pack's roar of approval at Farley's appearance.

"Good to see you out and about," Uncle Boris shouted.

"And you brought refreshments this time," another uncle added with approval.

No one approached Farley until Aunt Vera, the boldest wolf in the room, helped herself to one of his malty beverages. The pack swarmed in as Farley took the theft in stride.

Uncle Boris stepped up to him last and snagged a drink. Of course, a heavy wave of my uncle's pepper-spray-scented aftershave made Farley grimace.

"Boris, there are outhouses in the woods that smell better than the shit you put on," Farley griped.

Uncle Boris chuckled. "To the ladies, it's the nectar of the gods. I get you some. Get you back on the market."

"I'm good," Farley replied. "Y'all can help yourselves, but you need to save a cold one for me, you hear?"

That got laughter from the adults. I wanted to tell him to hold tight to one just in case, but Thorn snagged two out of the box.

With my father-in-law somewhat settled in, I had to greet Grandma. She sat on the sofa on the far side of the living room. Grandma Lasovskaya gave me a toothy grin, and her speckled brown eyes lit up when I knelt to greet her eye to eye. My grandma was older than every werewolf in here. A long time ago, she immigrated from Russia, and had lived to see many great landmarks like the Statue of Liberty being built.

"Are you hungry?" she asked.

"I'm starving. Do you need anything?"

She patted my hand with her wrinkled, warm one. "Return the whistle soon. I don't want you around those demons anymore."

"Don't worry." I touched the whistle in my pocket. "All of this will be over soon enough," I replied with a chuckle.

She slowly nodded, but her hand lingered on mine.

Concern flared in her eyes, and I wondered how much she knew about demons.

I left her to head into the kitchen to join Mom and Dad.

Dad glanced up from his seat at the kitchen table. I leaned down to kiss his cheek. The dark stubble tickled my lips. "Natalya, how did you manage to bring Farley?" he asked me in Russian.

"We tied him up and dragged him here," I joked.

That got a look of amusement from Dad; not so much from Mom.

"I'm surprised you got him to come," Mom said in English. "He never wanted to leave the cabin after Pearl died..." Mom's remarks trailed off as the man in question came into the kitchen with his beer. Guess he'd lost the box to someone. Thorn came up behind him.

Mom hid her embarrassment with a smile as she grabbed a plate. "We were excited to hear you'd come, Farley. There's plenty to eat if you're hungry." She added a full chicken to the plate and topped the meat with wild rice. She didn't wait for his protest.

"I could use some chow." Farley ambled to sit down.

Had he heard Mom's remark? If he had, he gave no sign.

Farley, Mom, Dad, and I sat at the four-seater table. Thorn leaned against the wall and slowly sipped his beer. Mom and I stole glances in his direction until Dad said in Russian, "He's not a wild animal. Let the man eat."

"Something wrong, Fyodor?" Farley asked.

"Your boy and his wife need to eat." Dad looked to Mom. "Anna, get these kids eating before they waste away to bones."

Mom got up and pushed Thorn to take her place to eat. While my mate and I attacked our food, Farley did the same, licking his fingers and humming with appreciation. The small smile at the corner of his mouth reminded me of the time when I'd received a warm welcome in this house again. Less than a year ago, I'd walked into this house as the pariah of the pack. Time passed, and when I returned, I wasn't a stranger anymore.

I tried not to imagine him sitting all alone in that cabin, but the image flared and my heart broke. Thorn had told me Farley had visitors now and then, but most of them were related to business matters. Sadly, I'd never dropped in to say hello or bring a plate of food. Who'd want to march into that messy hovel and come face to face with someone that reminded them of their weaknesses?

I let Farley eat in peace as the front door opened. The pack greeted the new arrivals, and I caught my brother's laugh in return.

Alexander Stravinsky, or Sasha as my family lovingly called him, and his family had arrived. My gaze flicked to Mom. If I hurried, I might be able to snag my niece before her grandma took over.

Mom put down her spoon, but her oven timer beeped.

Ha, saved by the buns.

Mom had to butter those too, so I had a couple of minutes.

In the living room, I spotted my brother's little family. I made a beeline for Karey and little Sveta. I'd seen Sasha enough growing up. Time to spoil my niece. I reached for her, and Karey surrendered her baby with a chuckle. At nine months old, Sveta continued to develop faster than a human. Since her father was a wolf and her mother a nymph, she'd have quite the interesting future.

"Where's Mom?" Karey asked, grabbing some covered dishes from Alex's hands. Based on the ghastly smell from within, Karey had made vegan fettuccine alfredo with almond milk and stinkhorn mushrooms again.

Hungry werewolves ate anything, but even we had limits.

"She's in the kitchen," I told her.

Then I turned to my niece and rained kisses on her cheeks. Little Sveta smelled like baby lotion and sunshine. I wish I could hold her all the time. "Did you miss me, *Printsessa?*"

I stuck to the living room until I heard Mom calling for me. My bonding time had come to an end. As alpha female, I couldn't pull rank over Mom when it came to her grandchild, but I could take my time… So I sashayed and danced my way to the kitchen. Sveta giggled and hopped against my hip.

Yep, we're taking our time to get to Grandma.

Once we reached the kitchen, my mom snatched Sveta and gave her only grandchild a sugar cookie. Like any feisty pup, the baby devoured the cookie in two chomps.

Karey followed us into the kitchen and placed her dishes on the table. She triumphantly uncovered them. Farley took one look, shuddered, and kept cramming wild rice into his mouth.

Mom, Karey, and I chatted for a bit. I loved the normalcy of hearing about Sveta growing out of her clothes and Karey's volunteer work in the state parks. If I hadn't spent the day searching for that damn whistle, it might've been any other evening with my family.

But it wasn't, and I couldn't forget that.

We continued to chat, but Sveta quickly got tired of her spot on Mom's hip. She squirmed and tried to escape. Even a cookie bribe from Grandma didn't keep that kid from her master escape plan. Mom kissed the top of her grandbaby's head and put her down. I reached for her, but my niece scampered past me to the kitchen table.

Dad's smile widened as his granddaughter climbed up on one of the seats.

"You want some help, sweetheart?" he asked gently in Russian.

The pup ignored him and pulled herself up like a professional climber. Dad and Thorn shifted plates aside to make room for her.

"Stop spoiling her, Fyodor," Mom chided.

"Hush, wife." Dad offered Sveta a bite of chicken, but the child shook her head.

Thorn chuckled at the sight. "That's not enough meat, Fyodor. Give her more."

All conversation in the room ceased as Sveta took a chicken bone from Farley's plate. The child used what little teeth she had to nibble on the bone.

"Svetlana, no!" Karey reached the table in two steps.

"Leave her be." Farley added another chicken leg bone to Sveta's other hand. "Will was the same way when his teeth were comin' in."

A sigh of relief slipped out of Mom. "Was Thorn that way too?"

Sveta got tired of nibbling on one of her bones and tried to use one to stir the vegan fettuccine alfredo, but Farley pushed the bowl to the side. "That boy was hunting down prey right out of the womb. Pearl always said he had a hunter's eye."

"Pearl would be proud of the fine men they've become," Mom said softly.

"She would be." Farley took a long look at Thorn.

My mate relaxed in his seat. Our gazes met, and the grin he gave me told me that this dinner had been good for everyone.

CHAPTER 19

Hiding Cerberus's whistle away gave me stress beyond measure, but then again, hadn't all the trials and tribulations I'd faced in the past prepared me for this moment? Night fell and morning arrived, bringing another day.

Today, as alpha female, I had to lead my pack to remember and mourn our fallen.

This morning the South Toms River Pack held a burial service for Francine Dalton at Mom and Dad's church. Pack members filled the pews, their heads lowered, words spoken at a whisper. Thorn and I paid our respects to the Dalton family, but no matter the condolences and words of encouragement, our words didn't feel like enough. Nothing would bring Francine back.

The only thing the family wanted was revenge.

After the service, we took Farley and Will home. I wanted to stay behind to spend time with the silent men, but I had something far more important to complete: I'd finally decided to fix up my former home for someone else.

Before we left my parents' place last night, I'd spoken to my mother and told her about my idea.

"I love it," she'd said. "But are you ready for this?"

"I'll never be ready, but I want to do the right thing."

She gave me a long mama bear hug, and she sprang into action late into the night, unleashing the power of the Stravinsky clan to help their own. Now all I had to do was follow through too.

Before I escaped to the cottage, I made a quick stop at the demon's mart to see if I could use an employee discount to fetch something that caught my eye not too long ago.

I pulled into the lot to find Dayla helping a customer load aquamarine planters into the back of their Subaru Outback. She waved when she spotted me.

"Good morning, Nat!" She gave me her usual bright smile. Today her white T-shirt featured a kitten buried in balls of rainbow-streaked yawn. I wondered if she hoarded those T-shirts or cats. Probably both.

"Hey, Dayla. I'm looking for a gift." I gestured to the beautiful stone wolf with a butterfly perched on its nose. "Any chance you'll sell that to me? I do understand if you can't since Mimi doesn't like me right now."

"Oh, Mimi can stuff it. Of course, you can buy it." She gave me a mischievous grin. "I won't tell her if you don't."

"Deal."

We walked inside and Dayla rang up my purchase.

"You look tired, Nat. You doing okay?" she asked as she took my money.

"It's been a long morning and the day hasn't started yet."

"Still looking for Mimi's whistle?" She walked around the counter to approach me with concern.

"Oh, I finally have it." I slowly shook my head. "She'll get it back soon enough."

Dayla pursed her lips and sighed with sympathy. "Let's

get you that wolf! You'll love it."

With the stone ornament packed into the back of my Nissan, I left the stone store ,and soon pulled up to my former home. Before I'd fought Erica and moved in with Thorn at his house across town, I'd lived here alone as the pariah of the South Toms River Pack. Remembering that time always felt like exposing an open wound to alcohol. I had wonderful memories here, but as I took in the forest surrounding the small two-story house, I wondered if this place could offer Farley a wall of protection from the outside world like it had for me.

Time to get to work.

With the whistle safely hidden away at home with additional security from the pack, I grabbed a shopping bag full of cleaning supplies and marched inside.

Not long into sorting the supplies into piles for each room, the Stravinskys arrived to offer a hand. Mom and Aunt Vera took over the kitchen. They set up a buffet table for the hungry wolves. My uncles and father set about tackling any pending inspections on the water heater and air-conditioning unit. More hardworking Stravinskys, consisting of my cousins, plowed through washing windows, linens, and curtains as Aggie arrived in Erica's BMW coupe with trays of pretty white daisies.

"How come you're in Erica's car? She couldn't come today?" I asked her as I helped unload the flowers from the trunk.

"She's not free today. She mentioned something about a date tonight." Aggie's reddish eyebrows waggled with mischief.

"A date?" Erica hadn't mentioned seeing anyone new. "Do you know who it is?"

"Nope. Hopefully she chose someone *outside* of town."

I nodded. The Stravinskys had plenty of bachelors, but I

wouldn't subject Erica to a lifetime of dealing with my family.

"By the way, where's the whistle?" Aggie asked.

"After we got home last night, I hid it in the one place no one *ever* checks."

I'd hidden the whistle in the bottom of a box of maxi-pads tucked at the back of the bathroom cabinet. In all the years I'd lived alone, only Aggie had picked up anything related to feminine hygiene products.

After we finished unloading the trays from the car, I helped Aggie plant the flowers along the walkway while my family and other pack members hauled care packages into the house. The Dalton butcher store truck arrived with meat to fill the freezer. Two pack families delivered bags with clothes to hang in the closets, while another added toiletries in the bathrooms.

I smiled all morning until Aggie paused in the middle of adding rows of daisies.

"There's something I need to say," she said.

I'd heard this tone of voice from her before and steeled myself for her remarks.

She tucked her wayward red hair behind her ear. "Nat, I know why you're doing this, and I commend you. Giving Farley your home is fucking amazing, but…"

"But?"

"I want you prepared in case Farley doesn't like this." Her face softened. "I care about you. He might walk out that door and shit on your efforts."

I sucked in a deep breath. "That's possible, but he might not do that."

She gave me a tight smile. "He might not, but Farley doesn't have a great track record of treating you well. Just be ready, okay?" She got up to wipe dirt off her jeans. "I need a snack. You want anything?"

"No thanks. I'm going to take care of the plastic bins on the driveway." As I hauled the bins containing the holiday cheer I'd hidden away in the house into the back of a mobile storage truck, I tried not to think of Aggie's words.

Farley will love this home.

Farley won't associate this place with me.

I told myself that Thorn's father and brother needed this home more than I did. And in order for Farley and me to move forward, one of us had to surrender.

Hopefully, Farley would accept a piece of my soul.

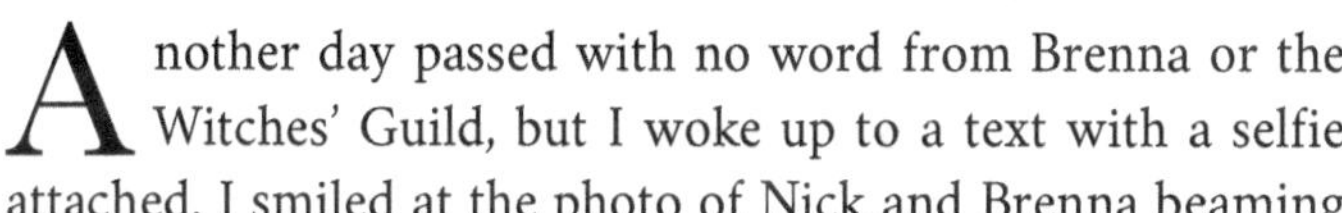

Another day passed with no word from Brenna or the Witches' Guild, but I woke up to a text with a selfie attached. I smiled at the photo of Nick and Brenna beaming from the waiting room of the warlock clinic.

Well done, Wizard, I texted back to him.

Now it was time for me to work on Dr. Frank's exercise too.

Thorn took the day off work and told Will on the downlow to do the same. We made a full breakfast as a couple, laughing while my mate fried up the hickory-smoked bacon and I used the stovetop griddle to craft heart-shaped pancakes. I even splurged and set out small bowls with chocolate chips, strawberries, and blueberry sauce. Of course, a pancake party wouldn't be complete without a can of whipped cream or a bowl of nuts.

Crashes and booms from a crime thriller floated out of the living room, but I knew Farley's stomach would drive him into the kitchen once we finished preparing the meal.

Thorn and I whizzed through the prep, setting the table and adding our dishes to complete the scene.

Will hovered near the doorway to the kitchen. "Everything smells amazing."

Farley poked his head around his son. "Get out of the way, Will."

Father and son hurried to the seats. Thorn and I exchanged a small smile. Time to line everything up for the big reveal.

Everyone filled their plates with buttered toast and pancakes overflowing with toppings, along with a piece of bacon or two. Then we sat. My heart rate shot up a notch as I plucked something from my pocket and placed it in my lap.

Across from me, Farley dug into his meal and Will had already inhaled his toast. The *clinks* and *clangs* of forks and knives hitting plates filled the room.

I peeked at Thorn. His eyebrows rose.

It was now or never.

I slid a key with a red ribbon tied to it across the table to Farley.

"What's that?" His face lit up. "You got me a car?"

Whoops.

"This key opens the door to something far more valuable," Thorn said slowly.

Farley put down his fork. "You found a place?"

Thorn and I nodded.

"Natalya helped us," Thorn added.

After hearing that, Farley sat still for a moment. I couldn't read his face. Suddenly, Farley ambled to stand.

My gaze flicked to Thorn's fallen face. He shrugged.

"Why are we still eating, boy?" Farley grumbled.

Will paused in the middle of a bite. "'Cause we're hungry?"

"Let's go." Farley snatched the key and abandoned his food.

Ten minutes later, anxiety swallowed my anticipation

whole. Farley's face turned to a scowl as we pulled up to my former home. The daisies Aggie and I had planted along the walkway up to the house stood tall. A pleasant breeze rocked the nearby evergreen and oak trees, almost beckoning us to explore the woods beyond. I couldn't have expected a better sunny day for us to show up.

Thorn, Will, and I left the car first. It took a single inhale and exhale for Farley to follow us. He lingered outside the car before he examined the daisies, then checked out the brand-new WELCOME HOME doormat near the door. No one spoke while we circled the house.

I tried to read his body language and scent. What did he think? What did he feel?

We waited patiently until Farley used the key to unlock the door, then he limped inside. The cool air in the living room embraced us. I swallowed past the lump in my throat as Farley's gaze swept over the room.

Everything appeared picturesque. My old furniture was inviting, and the freshly laundered curtains were open to let the mid-July sunshine fill the room. The brand-new La-Z-Boy Uncle Boris hauled into the room had navy-blue pillows arranged just right. On the other side of the room, Dad had placed the TV from my parents' bedroom on a stand I found at The Bends. Even the framed photos from the Grantham cabin placed here and there added charm to a beautiful room.

But what did Farley think?

Farley's silent examination ended with the items placed in the middle of the living room coffee table. He stared hard at the three black walnut blocks, as well as the kit with a carving chisel, whittling knife, and carving gouge.

Thorn shoved his hands into the pockets of blue jeans. "Do you like it, Dad?"

Farley strolled over to the new framed photo of Pearl

holding her figurines. Briefly, he touched the picture.

Before I could stay quiet, I added, "If you don't like it, we can move things around. Or buy you a better TV."

My father-in-law's face tightened, and wrinkles gathered on his brow. The straight line of his mouth deepened into a scowl.

"I'm tired of his bullshit." Will slipped from the house, slamming the door behind him.

Thorn opened his mouth to speak, but I gently placed my hand on his shoulder.

The Grantham men had fought enough, but Thorn refused to back down this time.

"The pack and my wife worked hard to make a new home for you," he said firmly. "Don't you have anything to say?"

Farley jerked his chin at the carving kit. "I need a home, but I don't want any reminders—"

"Reminders of what? That she's not coming back?" Thorn picked up a frame off the mantel. "I miss Mom too, but you shouldn't treat us this way. Right after she was killed, I wanted to destroy the world with you. As a kid, I wanted her to come home more than anything, but over time I learned that wasn't possible. She'd want you to live a good life."

Farley's lip curled. "You don't know shit, boy. You still have Natalya."

I lowered my head at the mention of my name.

Farley continued. "Have you ever loved someone so deep you couldn't imagine anyone replacing them? When that rogue wolf killed her, I thought I'd feel better after I put that animal down and buried his bones, but I still feel hollow."

"We don't want you to feel that way," Thorn said. "You're not alone anymore. We don't want you to be alone."

Farley presented his back to us and didn't turn around. "Maybe I'd rather be alone than see her every time I look at you."

CHAPTER 20

Thorn and I hoped Farley would spend the night in his new home, but without an explanation given, he returned home with us. The family spent a tense Friday night in separate rooms until Saturday morning arrived.

The worry from keeping the whistle safe only amplified my fears.

Every day, I'd kept my phone close while I waited for Brenna's reply. Not long into the afternoon, I got the text I was waiting for: *We're on our way to South Toms River to escort you to the night demon. Be ready to move with the whistle once we arrive.*

I read the message twice, but I clearly understood: the witches wanted me to surrender the whistle to the demon. As to why the whistle posed a danger, I wanted to know. Instead of stiffly replying "why," I forced myself to throw on a white T-shirt, jeans, and a pair of running shoes. Then I fished out the whistle from its hiding place and stuffed it into a backpack. With my goblin blade tucked into a knife holder on my ankle, I felt ready to meet the spellcasters once they arrived.

Farley spotted me making final preparations. After my disastrous attempt to give him my home, I was surprised to hear him blurt out, "Is it time to return the whistle to those damn demons?"

"Yes."

"About time. I was nervous having it around the house." After he swallowed deeply a couple of times, he added, "Be careful. I can't have you getting hurt and worrying Thorn and such."

I'd worry Thorn, but not him, huh?

I can't win the war in a day.

Time to wait for the spellcasters. I peeked through the living room window to the outside. So far the day promised a dreary day with gray sky, rain, and a brisk wind. I scanned the yard for any trouble. The wind's howls made it difficult to listen for any oncoming danger, but I nonetheless stood on the porch and checked on our lookouts. Yesterday my brother Alex and one of his best friends kept guard, then, right before dinnertime, Rex's younger brothers took over. Only two cars sat fifteen feet away on along our driveway: Melvin's Chevy Impala and my Nissan Altima. No one stood watch inside or around Melvin's vehicle.

Fear pricked my spine.

They're fine, they're fine. You're the master of assumptions. Don't let your head get the best of you.

I searched the tree line but found nothing. Damn, where were those guys? I donned a black raincoat, slung the backpack over my shoulder, and walked out as far as necessary to check the Impala. Maybe Rex's brothers were fast asleep in the back seat.

I crept to the car, finding the seats empty, and the driver's door was slightly ajar.

Not good.

I backed up toward the house. Of course, the goblin blade fluttered against my ankle in dire warning.

Shit. Shit. Shit.

I plucked out the weapon with one hand and grasped my phone with the other. I pressed the home button and said into the phone, "Send a text to Thorn Grantham: SOS at home!"

The tree line shuddered to my left, then right. The goblin blade rattled in my hands and stretched out to become the spiked shield again. My stomach plopped to my feet. Seconds from a full-out panic attack, I turned around and raced toward the house. Heavy footsteps stomped up the driveway. I kept my eyes on the doorway.

Brace yourself in the house. Wait for backup.

But the moment I reached the porch, I knew I wouldn't make it. Predators can also be prey. We feel the hairs tingle on the backs of our necks. Our breaths go from hitches to held.

I snapped around and braced myself behind the shield. My oncoming attacker slammed into me. I fought back a curse as I held the line Gandalf-style until I was swept off my feet. The shield smacked my face. My back careened through the front door and the world spun as I rolled into the house.

Get up, Nat. The door's wide open.

Blood filled my mouth. A horrific ache in my shoulder rose to alarming levels. From afar, I caught the sounds of the doorframe cracking, then exploding as someone burst through. More heavy footsteps approached fast. The temperature in the room dropped to freezing.

"What's going on!" Farley yelled.

I ignored him, got up, and braced myself again. Another blow hammered against the shield. Bits of flaming thorns from the shield fell to the floor. My attacker's height stretched beyond the seven-foot-high ceiling, forcing it to crouch. I peered up to see a skeletal man with strands of green hair and milky skin. His hair swayed like willow branches. With each foul exhale, the creature hit the top of my head with a frigid breath. His pink-hued stones for eyes stared daggers at me as he drew back his fist and punched the shield again. The flames bit at his skin, but the fire had no effect.

Good God, it's a frost giant. Where's the other one?

From across the room, shots rang out. I twisted to see Farley firing the Colt Navy Revolver. His rounds pelted the frost giant's side, forcing the creature to shield its eyes with its forearm. Bits of ice shards fell off its body.

Suddenly, the front window shattered, and a blur leapt into the living room. The dark form careened into my father-in-law.

"Farley!" My call to him was swallowed away as the frost giant snatched the edge of my shield and yanked backward.

Rage gathered in my chest. My claws extended and my roar bounced off the walls.

The frost giant wrenched my shield away and tossed it down the hallway. With a grunt, it swung at me again, but I dodged the blow and scampered toward Farley—only to come face to face with a black-and-white wolflike creature. It crept toward me, its mouth wide open with ice shards for teeth and speckled sunstones for eyes.

I bared my teeth back at it, ready to fight if necessary. If it hurt Farley…

I crouched, ready to spring forward, but the frost giant grabbed my backpack. With a single touch from the giant, the fabric on the pack gave way. The whistle fell to the floor with a *clink* and rolled to the far wall. I scrambled to go after it, but the frost wolf sprang on me and bit my wounded shoulder.

I screamed in pain, and the whole world went white. Then black.

The beast held me tight and shook me hard. A scalding burn snaked toward the middle of my chest, and the pain stabbed my lungs with ice-cold needles. I waited for my heart to stop, but the frost wolf released me and escaped out of what was left of the front door.

Heat swept through the room again, but I was too busy clawing at each precious inhale. My breath came out in dry gasps, but I willed myself to fight as my lungs seized repeatedly. I forced myself to roll over.

I had to find Farley.

Inch by inch, I crawled my way to the turned-over La-Z-Boy. I blacked out twice, but I managed to find him lying among the broken window's shattered bits and what was left of the end table next to the recliner.

Thorn's father let out a mewling moan as he clutched his stomach.

"Are you okay?" I examined him for any other bites or wounds.

He rolled up his shirt to reveal a large spot darkening from pink to a splotchy red.

"Oh shit. Stay still," I said. Every breath came out as a wheeze.

"No." He pushed me away. "Find the whistle."

Oh, no.

I flopped around until I wobbled to a sitting position. From there I precariously scooted across the living room toward the last place I'd seen the whistle. I searched along the wall, the harsh sound of my wheezes growing louder as my panic returned.

The whistle was gone, and our uninvited guests had escaped.

I got to my feet and staggered to the doorway. Right

before I crossed the threshold, my vision swam and I collapsed. The grumble of approaching cars careening up the driveway was the last thing I heard.

CHAPTER 21

Not long after Thorn and the cavalry arrived, Brenna and Nick showed up too. From where I lay in Thorn's arms in one corner, I watched the pair enter the house. Around us, pack members swarmed about and focused on cleaning up the mess. Those with carpentry skills tried to repair the doorframe, while my brother vacuumed up the glass and my dad covered up the broken window with plastic.

The earth witch took one long look at me and her face softened. Even Nick shook his head.

"Should I tell the spellcasters we won the fight?" I whispered weakly to Thorn.

He laughed. "I can't believe you're making jokes at a time like this."

The spellcasters weaved around everyone and joined us. Water dripped from Brenna's lime-green raincoat onto the carpet, but I didn't care. As usual, the wizard didn't have a drop of rain on him.

"I wish we'd left sooner." Nick knelt next to us and looked me over. "Is anyone else badly injured?"

"Go check on Farley." I could barely breathe through the pain in my chest, but at least I clung to consciousness. Poor Farley had blacked out a couple times.

"Are you sure about this?" Thorn asked. "I can smell your pain."

Even Nick hesitated, but after I nodded, the wizard left my side to check on my father-in-law.

"You look horrible," Brenna said. She got up and brought me a blanket. I was far too hot to need it, but I appreciated the gesture. "Are you sure I can't make you more comfortable?" she asked.

"Comfortable isn't in my vocabulary anymore." I snorted, then grimaced.

"What attacked you?" she asked. "Was it the creatures that killed Francine Dalton?"

"It was a frost giant and frost wolf." I held my breath to keep the sharp pain at bay for a moment and failed.

"Rest and answer questions later," Thorn warned me.

I chuckled and winced. At least my pain hadn't worsened, but if the frost wolf had burned me like last time, I was in for worse pain later. "Start stocking up on those smoothies," I said to Brenna. "After all this is over, I want a couple bottles, if possible."

She smiled and leaned in. "You got it."

A couple minutes later, I heard an annoyed grunt, then Farley snapped, "How much longer do you have to touch me, Wizard?"

I rolled my eyes. At least his complaints were a good sign.

"Dad, lie still," Will said with annoyance. Thorn's younger brother apologized profusely to Nick, but Farley kept yapping on about how he didn't want any help from them dirty, underhanded spellcastin' folks.

"Sorry you had to hear that," I whispered to Brenna.

She shook her head. "I've heard worse."

By the time Nick strode over to me, Farley was up. I was pleasantly surprised to see him walk without a limp throughout the room, the antique gun tucked into the back of his trousers.

And he waltzed around the pack members without a care. The Code be damned.

What I still needed to know was where did he get the bullets?

"Did anyone see where they went?" Farley growled. "And what happened to our guards?"

"Melvin and Benny went out to…relieve themselves. They came back. We sent them out to follow their tracks. They're should report back to us soon," my dad explained to him.

"Them two idiots couldn't defend an abandoned Taco Bell," Farley drawled.

Nick stooped next to me and sighed. "This has been an interesting morning."

"Oh God, yes," I agreed.

"You and I were supposed to regale Dr. Frank with progress after we dropped off the whistle." He gently pressed his hand to my shoulder. The soothing warmth of his healing seeped into me. "I planned to talk about how I healed a warlock or two, which I begrudgingly did after I took the picture I sent you, and you were supposed to talk about your gift giving. How did that go, by the way?"

I wanted to shrug but voted down that idea. "I picked the wrong gift. Maybe I'll lie to our therapist and say we had a heart-to-heart with sunshine and rainbows."

Brenna giggled. "I don't know about you, but Farley found the gun useful."

"Useful, yes, but heartfelt, no. I gave him another gift, but that didn't work either." The pain in my shoulder lessened, and soon every exhale didn't feel like I'd inhaled shards of glass.

"We should've kept the whistle for you," Nick said firmly.

Brenna nodded in agreement.

"It was my responsibility to return it," I said. "Anything could've happened. For all we know, the frost giant would've attacked you two, and I…"

"And you what?" Brenna said with a growing grin.

"And I would've felt bad, since I kinda like you guys," I finished.

She patted my arm and turned to Nick. "Do you need a boost in energy? I'm going to get her a drink."

Seeing the adoration in her eyes made me smile inside. I wanted someone to look at Nick the way he used to look at me.

"No need to help," Nick said. "I brought a wand I can tap into today."

"I'm glad to hear about your time in the clinic," I remarked.

"Spending time there wasn't easy, but then again, growth can be painful." He looked over his shoulder at Brenna as she filled a cup with tap water. "I hated every minute of it, and Brenna was patient."

I tapped his hand that grasped my shoulder. "I'm glad she was there for you, Fenton. Okay, I'm good now." I gently pushed Nick away. With renewed strength in my limbs, I eased myself up and tested out my shoulder. "Farley looks like his normal grumpy self again," I said. "Will he be all right?"

"I patched up his broken ribs," Nick said, "so he's in much better shape now. Actually, much better than fine." Nick winked at Thorn and me. "I fixed a couple of ailments that have slowed him down, but we'll keep that a secret until he notices."

"Did you fix his attitude?" I asked dryly.

Nick chuckled a little. "I'm afraid psychiatry isn't in my bag of tricks."

When I turned to check on Farley, the stubborn wolf showed no signs of lingering pain. He stood next to the door and stared out to the woods.

Thorn and I joined him.

"Come sit down, Dad," Thorn said.

"Not today, boy." Farley jerked his chin to the woods. "If them monsters want to come knockin' on my door, I mean to return the favor."

"I want to find them too, but we don't know their location…yet," Thorn replied.

"We don't need to know." Farley glanced at me. A fire that I hadn't seen before shone in his blue eyes. "When I visited the Daltons the other day, they told me they'd noticed missing food two days prior to the attack."

"Really?" I asked.

"That means the frost wolf needs to feed every couple of days," Thorn said.

Farley's scowl deepened. "I say we lure them out with some chow. And when that mutt comes sniffing around, the giant will have to follow. Then we separate them and take them out one by one."

Thorn's brow furrowed. "I don't like this idea. One strike from either of them can debilitate us. It's a half-moon tonight, and the pack won't be at full strength."

"Don't matter." Farley's voice rose until the other pack members turned to listen. "They came into your house and attacked our pack. If we don't retaliate, this isn't your territory anymore. It's theirs."

∼

Seeing my father-in-law stand tall and walking among us lit a fire in the pack members' bellies. Many pack members drew closer to listen. Back when Farley led the pack with his injuries, he'd always barked orders from the cabin, making appearances when necessary. Now that Farley stood among us with his back straight and his leg fixed, he was eager to fight, but it was Thorn who reined us in to form a plan before we leapt into the fray.

A couple hours later, Rex reported that Melvin and Benny still followed the pair along the northern edge of Double Trouble State Park. A buzz grew among the gathered pack members. The rain restarted with a light drizzle, but many men and women waited outside in the warm rain. Anger radiated off a few, while fear drenched many as much as the rainy weather. After Francine's death, I sensed a hunger for vengeance.

"You need to sit down and rest," Thorn advised me. "We plan to attack after the sun sets."

I craved another Natalya-burrito-sleep-a-thon, but I could wait. "I'll rest tonight after we get the whistle back."

Even the spellcasters waited on the porch while Frank and Bella Dalton showed up in their delivery truck with enough meat to lure our target. Once we could predict where the pair planned to go, we'd leave. I glanced up toward the sky. Mother moon hid behind the gray clouds, her pull distant.

I walked up to Brenna and Nick. The pair held up the wall on the other side of the porch. "I wouldn't feel hurt if you two disappeared before things went down. I wouldn't want you to get hurt."

"Does she always do this?" Brenna asked.

"I told you she'd say it," Nick replied.

I looked between the two. Did I miss something?

"Yeah, he told me earlier you'd try to drive us away," Brenna admitted. "I bet a couple bucks you'd try to lure us away. He said you'd outright tell us."

I rolled my eyes. "How much did you win?"

"Should I tell her?" Brenna's teasing eyes told me she'd enjoy her spoils.

"No." Nick shook his head with a small smile.

She turned to me. "Frost giants are dangerous. You'll need all the help you can get. The forest is my territory too. You'll need every advantage."

She had a point there.

By the time the sun set, many more pack members had arrived from work. Aggie and Erica pulled up ready to kick some ass. Aggie waltzed up to me while Erica veered off to check on Farley.

"How was work?" I asked Aggie.

"Are you seriously asking me about work after what happened?"

"At this point, I'd rather talk about anything other than fighting a frost giant."

She pursed her lips at me and tugged me into a hug. "When all this is over, we need to have another girls' night out."

I snorted. "Next time I get to pick the movies."

She released me and grinned. "Nope, my house, my rules."

"Erica is invited too, right?"

"If she isn't busy with her new man, we can." A hint of envy flashed in Aggie's eyes, but when Erica walked up to us, I knew everyone was good.

"I heard you got hurt," she said to me. "How are you feeling?"

"Much better than earlier," I replied. "Farley and I got our asses handed to us, but Nick helped us out."

"What are we up against?" Aggie asked.

I updated them on what had happened so far with finding the whistle, my unfortunate deal with the leprechaun, and then losing the whistle again to the frost giant.

"Why did the giant steal the whistle?" Erica asked.

"That's a question I still can't answer." I shook my head.

Erica nodded as she chewed on the thought. "Why isn't the frost giant chasing after those fairies in New York? What's it doing lurking around here?"

I squared my shoulders. "If we catch it, I plan to find out."

CHAPTER 22

More ominous clouds gathered as pack members assembled in the Double Trouble State Park parking lot. Rows and rows of vehicles, trucks, SUVs, and even campers lined the space. The park closed after dark, but with a pack member working as a park ranger, we arranged for the pack to sneak inside.

Using intel from Melvin and Benny, we learned the pair was heading south—which meant we could trap them. The Daltons and a couple other pack members raced south around the park and found an interception point to plant the meat to draw the wolf. We also had spare clothes, and the goblin blade was stowed away in the SUV.

Now, all we had to do was attack them and retrieve the whistle.

Briefly, I took in my friends' and family's faces. Aggie and Erica were stoic—far too calm for what was about to take place. My parents had fought many battles, but before each one, they always hugged, and Dad kissed her forehead like he did every morning before he went to work. The spellcasters spoke among themselves, their expressions serious and their hands gesturing as if they were strategizing. Other pack members like Bella Dalton paced and fidgeted. Eagerness to begin the hunt shone in her eyes. Bella, in particular, wanted to take down the frost wolf to avenge her sister's murder.

But it was Farley who separated from the pack and lingered at the edge of the trees. He stared out into the woods and never moved.

"Will he be all right?" I asked Thorn.

"He hasn't fought in a long time." Briefly, he cradled my cheek with his warm palm. "I'd say he's more than all right. Are you ready?"

"Of course. This is gonna be great." I rubbed where the frost wolf had bitten me.

Thorn smelled through my lie and chuckled. "You're one of the strongest people I know. Just keep everyone together and you'll be fine."

Once everyone had their instructions, Nick and Brenna departed first to head to the rendezvous point. Around me, pack members shed their clothes to shift. I did the same and let nature take its course. Changing from a human into a wolf wasn't shapeshifting into a new form, but a transformation into the body we were meant to be within. And that change came with pain, like childbirth. Thankfully, I'd discovered that as I grew older, the transformation became less painful.

Pack members yipped around me, gleeful as the night revealed its secrets through scents and sounds the humans couldn't hear. A herd of whitetail deer had run through here recently, and foraging cottontails emerged from their dens. The wolf within wanted to follow the deer, but we had work to do.

Thorn's gray-and-black form darted ahead as rain began to fall. He circled back to bring the pack together with barks and nips at our heels. Time to move. He set off with a brisk pace into the forest. We followed. Running with the pack always left me buoyant, but this time the desire to tear apart our enemies circled my stomach. That desire grew tenfold as the coppery scent of raw meat grew overpowering. We were close to our rendezvous point.

I wasn't sure how much time passed, but soon we entered the clearing for our trap. Pack members eyed the food, with some even daring to investigate, but Thorn and I kept them back and herded the wolves into two groups. The spell-casters arrived and took their position to the south. Thorn and Farley, along with my kin, disappeared into the trees to the west, while I took another group with Erica, Bella, Aggie, and others to the east.

Then we waited. No one made a sound.

I stared through the woods at the meat trap. The Daltons had left rather tasty-looking cuts of beef and pork, and someone had even tossed in some shriveled-up beef jerky.

Rain continued to fall, but I didn't shake off the water. My gaze never left the spot.

I wanted another opportunity to face down the frost giant. I had too many questions to answer. In particular, where did those two come from?

Minutes transformed into an hour. The muscles in my legs groaned in protest, but I stayed still and the others around me did the same. Our patience paid off when a single form shot out into the clearing from the north and made a beeline for the chow. The frost wolf dove into the pile and gobbled up a couple of morsels. I expected the frost giant to join his companion, but the creature waited at the edge of the clearing, his body tense and eyes searching into the woods.

Now that I could see the giant clearly, I noticed it wore dirty trousers, but no shirt. Was the whistle hidden in one of its pockets? The giant took a tentative step into the clearing as rain flattened his willow-branch-like hair against his scalp.

The clouds parted, and moonlight flooded the clearing. Something glinted on the giant's ankle. I peered harder, noticing a strap of ivy wrapped around the ankle with a sunstone bead strung on it.

No way.

Did this thing belong to one of the demons?

I must've moved, because Aggie nipped at my neck.

No, her blue eyes seemed to convey.

But I had to see. During the fight, I'd worried for my life and hadn't considered all these details. The frost giant had fingernails made of buckeye seed and piercing sunstone eyes. Did all these represent "day" things? Mademoiselle Midnight's creation didn't have the same composition as this one.

Dread soured my stomach as another idea came to mind: had Dayla created the frost giant and the frost wolf?

And if that was true, why?

I didn't have a moment to figure out an answer when the frost giant grunted at the wolf. Then he traced the shape of an axe on his chest. Before my very eyes, the tracing formed an obsidian axe. The giant grasped it and turned his head to focus on Thorn's position. He'd spotted them.

My stomach jumped to my throat.

Be careful, Thorn.

The frost wolf circled the food twice, eager to eat, and ignored its companion's command.

From the other side of the clearing, a yip filled the air. A rush filled my belly as Thorn broke out of the woods and sped toward the nearest target: the frost giant. Ten feet to the right of Thorn's group, bushes and trees parted to reveal the hidden spellcasters.

I took a step toward the frost wolf, and my group prepared to sprint. We tore out of the woods and ran hard, cutting off the frost wolf's path back to the giant.

Gotcha.

With the frost wolf isolated, we sprang into action.

I encountered the frost wolf first, ramming its side. Aggie came at next, her mouth open wide for its neck. Once she pounced, we all jumped in for the kill. I sank my teeth into its flank, and at first, its flesh didn't yield, but when I clamped down, my teeth sank in deep.

The frost wolf's frigid teeth bit into my leg, forcing me to retreat, but I tasted victory and jumped back into the fray. Our adversary tried to run away, but Bella leapt forward and blocked its path. The animal came at her, clawing at her snout while we surrounded it.

Come on, you slippery bastard.

Not far from us, the ground shook. Bright lights and thunderclaps filled the clearing. I hoped the others fared well with the giant.

Through an unspoken word from me, we attacked again as one. We clamped down on it. Teared it. Clawed at it. Our frenzy rose to a fevered pitch until I was heady. Moments later, the frost wolf collapsed with Bella at its neck. When we backed away, the frost wolf lay dead.

I poked it with my snout, just to be sure.

We circled our fallen foe, but we didn't linger long. The other group needed us. We broke away from the frost wolf to race toward the light. My speed picked up again. My leg bite throbbed and the wound opened more, but I ignored the pain and set my gaze on the next the frost giant.

On the other side of the field, the spellcasters and wolves couldn't break through the frost giant's defenses. Armed with his frost axe, the giant swung at anyone who got too close.

Nick advanced from the south, extending a glowing white staff toward the heavens. Lightning danced from cloud to cloud before it raced to the tip of the staff, then slammed into the giant. The white heat bounced off the giant's shoulders, leaving him unharmed.

Meanwhile, Brenna, with her oak wand in hand, crept toward the giant from the southeast. The tall grass parted and writhed with her passage. What did she plan to do?

We were almost there as Thorn's group circled for another attack.

From Nick's position, I faintly heard him yell, "Not yet!"

But it was too late. We'd gotten too close. The frost giant's sunstone eyes changed from speckled pink to burnt orange. He sucked in a deep breath and raised his axe in the air. When the frost giant slammed the obsidian axe to the ground, a shimmering wave fluttered through the rainfall and spread outward like a tsunami. Brenna raced to hide behind a rock formation she summoned while Nick's staff absorbed the blow. The ripple hit me and flung me back. The wolves around me yowled as they were tossed into the trees.

I landed hard on my back, but I shook off the jolt to see Nick toss his burned staff to the ground. Brenna advanced again.

Were Thorn and Farley okay? I searched for them until I spotted father and son preparing for another attack. Beside me, Aggie gingerly stood, shook her head, then bumped her flank against mine. Bella and Erica took longer to get to their feet.

We had little time to recover.

I hurried back into the fight. Behind me, Aggie, Bella, Erica, and my group picked up the pace.

Across the field, Nick launched fireballs from a mahogany wand. Smoldering rocks screamed as they sailed across the clearing. The blasts bounced off the giant like pebbles.

Mademoiselle Midnight's message to me rang loud and

clear: *Another artifact was taken last night. It was a beaded jade bracelet used to protect the wearer from incredible heat.*

If the frost giant had that jade bracelet, none of those attacks would help.

More pack members tried to sweep in, but the frost giant's axe knocked them back.

"Buy me some time!" Brenna advanced again. Trees in the clearing began to flutter, their branches swaying against the direction of the rain and wind.

"It never sounds good when you say that," Nick snapped back.

If I could speak, I would've told them to fight first and argue later.

Brenna crept ever closer as Thorn's group came from the east and I charged from the west. Before we pounced him as one, thick tree roots shot out of the ground at the frost giant's feet. The muddy roots snaked around his ankles and clamped his wrists together. The axe fell to the ground with a heavy thump. The earth witch clenched her teeth, her hands forming fists as if she held the giant in place with sheer will. She edged toward the giant—but got too close, and the giant's hand shot out to snatch her neck.

"Brenna!" Nick called out.

The pack swarmed the frost giant, sinking our teeth into his legs, arms, and neck. The giant swayed to the left, teetering and wobbling like a pendulum. We clung to it, growling and shaking it to free Brenna. As the frost giant careened to the right with Thorn at the giant's neck, our adversary's grip around Brenna's neck relaxed, and the giant fell.

Nick ran to Brenna and dragged her back. The frost giant released a long moan. The sound cut off as Thorn made the killing blow. After that, the only sound that remained in the field was suffering. The fallen wolves cried out. Brenna lay limp while Erica and Aggie circled the poor earth witch. Soon enough Nick would heal her, but many others needed him too.

I checked my mate first, finding him bloody, but unharmed. Poor old Farley had a limp again from a blow to his right leg. He continued to stalk the frost giant's body. I ran from wolf to wolf, seeing to everyone's well-being before I returned to Thorn, who lurked near the fallen giant. Thorn tried to nudge me away in case of danger, but I had to find the whistle. First, I examined our foe, from the sunflower seeds that peppered his face like freckles to the outline on his chest where his axe tattoo was inked. This creature appeared far more powerful than the night guard I'd seen. I patted the frost giant's pockets for the whistle. Nothing. I searched around the body, but the whistle wasn't here either. Dejected, I plopped down to finally catch my breath.

Minutes later, Thorn appeared in human form with clothing the Dalton family had left for us. He placed a shirt and shorts at my feet. "Take your time."

I should've rested a bit more, but as I returned to human form and got dressed, all the pieces of the puzzle slipped together.

"I know where the whistle is," I said.

The other pack members converged to my position near the fallen giant. Already his skin had turned dark gray like the dead night guard. Bit by bit, the frost giant began to melt away.

"Is it in the park somewhere? Erica asked. "Do you think the giant hid it out here?"

I shook my head. "That frost giant and the frost wolf came in from the north. I'd bet money they came from town."

Farley's brow knotted. "And where did they go while they were in town?"

Before I answered that question, I told them about the

similarities between the frost giant and the night guard: from their ivy ankle bracelets to the natural materials used to compose them. Then I made the next jump. If the night demon created the night guard from night materials, then another demon created the frost giant.

"You believe the day demon made that?" Aggie asked. "Why would she unleash that thing on the town? Why kill her customers?"

"I don't think her overall goal was to kill us," I said. "I believe the true party behind all of this is the day demon. She wanted the fairies to have the whistle and to use it. The attacks in Manhattan ended once the fairies lost it. After that, the frost giant lurked around town, but didn't make its presence known until I retrieved the whistle. Then Dayla's minions came after me and got her property back."

"What will she do with it?" Thorn asked.

"She'll blow it to summon Cerberus," I said.

"Why on earth would anyone do that?" Aggie asked.

"I'm not sure why yet," I admitted. "But I plan to see Dayla in the morning and find out."

Now that the fight had ended, pack members helped the wounded to their cars. Nick healed as many as he could before he grew too weak and had to go home with Brenna. Yet again, my good friend supported me in my time of need. I hoped to return the favor sooner rather than later.

Once the wounded were safely on the way home, the able-bodied pack members hauled the meat back into the truck for disposal. By this point, my leg throbbed from the bite, and my desire to wash away the filth from the forest became unbearable.

But we had more work to do, namely burying our foes' bodies if anything remained. I checked on the frost wolf and found the animal as nothing more than a pile of pine quills, two sunstones, and melted ice. The frost giant appeared to have melted too down to its ingredients, but twenty tiny beads glinted from the pile. I'd found the missing bracelet, but no cord to tie the pieces together. Eh, I'd make the night demon happy with something rather than nothing.

Thorn and I waited until everyone left. All that remained included my parents and the Daltons. We headed to Thorn's car to leave the park, but we couldn't find his SUV.

"Who had the keys?" I asked.

"My dad had them." Thorn scratched his head. "Did he forget about us?"

"He said nothing about leaving early." My mate and I stared at each other briefly.

"Maybe he got tired and giving us a ride home slipped his mind."

"Or he went to see the day demon to strike a deal," I said slowly.

"I thought you said the day demon sleeps during the day."

"Are we sure about that? I'm not."

Thorn nodded in agreement.

My stomach tied into never-ending knots. "We need to find him before he gets himself killed."

CHAPTER 23

We borrowed my dad's truck and searched a couple of places like the local convenience stores and a pub or two. Farley hadn't returned to his new home at my old house either.

It was time to check the ceramic mart.

As we arrived in the parking lot, pulling up next to the BMW Coupe Aggie and Erica waited in, I peered into the store, hoping to see Farley speaking with Dayla, but the store's interior appeared dim and empty.

Thorn got out of the truck first. "I can smell his aftershave."

Erica and Aggie followed Thorn. I limped along after them.

We tracked Farley's scent from the SUV up to the metal fencing. Nothing stirred among the stone figurines or the piles of marble and cut granite. We jumped over the fence and headed to the front door. Unfortunately, it was locked.

"Is there any other way inside?" Thorn asked. "A back door?"

"This is the only way." I bit my lower lip. "There is a back door, but it's a magical one that leads to the Midnight Barge. I don't know if it goes both ways."

We scanned the interior again. Beside me, Thorn's fury rose. I touched his arms.

"I know he's in there," Thorn growled.

I wasn't convinced Farley had made it inside to speak with Dayla, but we had to know. I touched the window, and a spark bit my palm.

"There are defensive measures around here." I motioned for the others to follow me around the store. "Let's try to see if we can find the night demon. Maybe she can sneak us inside."

We hurried to the back. My friends and mate came to a stop.

"There's nothing here," Erica said.

"I do see dead fish and cigarette butts," Aggie added.

None of them could see the thick fog or the dimmed lanterns from the Midnight Barge.

"Follow me." I directed Thorn to place his hand on my shoulder. We formed a chain and carefully made our way to the Midnight Barge.

Limping hard on my bitten leg, I led the others up the gangplank. Once everyone set foot onto the boat, their eyes widened.

"This is unreal," Aggie breathed.

The amber, green, and lavender lights along the deck fencing cast an unearthly glow and pushed away the darkest shadows. The faint tinkle of a harpsichord playing a soft tune reached my ears. A night spirit or two hovered near me with their purchases, but I told them to go to the register on the other side of the boat. Hopefully, there would be someone there to take care of them.

"What kind of store is this?" Erica asked.

Mademoiselle Midnight materialized in front of us. "It's a

rare antique store for night spirits and other creatures of the dark and deep."

Thorn shuffled back a step.

"Why are you here, Noelle?" the night demon asked. "Do you have my whistle?"

I sighed. "I don't have it."

The starlight in her hair glittered like tiny, brilliant supernovas. "Do you mock me, Wolf?"

My mate growled and my friends stiffened. I couldn't let this escalate. I stepped between them and the night demon.

"I know who took it." My gaze briefly touched the nearby ceramic mart. "Is there a place where we can speak in private?"

That made Mimi pause, but she motioned for me to follow her. We made our way through the Main Deck until we reached the upward staircase to the Hurricane Deck. We followed her up two sets of stairs to the final floor. At the top, the doorway to the night demon's quarters opened with a groan. Bright lights beckoned us into a chamber far larger than what I'd seen from the riverbank. More lanterns, far too many for me to count, hung from the vaulted ceiling. They dipped and hovered like nervous fireflies. Mimi's personal space included a sitting area to the right, her sleeping quarters in the center, and to the left I discovered what had to be where she kept her collection of night things. Pots of nightshade, ferns, and night-blooming moonflowers grew in pots on one table, while on another, she had bowls of poisonous berries harvested from bushes growing from larger containers.

Erica ran her fingers along a set of polished animal horns with appreciation.

"Those came from Tibetan night elk," the night demon explained.

"I wish I could see one someday," Erica replied.

"It's taken me centuries to find many of them." She directed us to a sitting area with wooden chairs covered in sheep's wool.

Instead of a rug under our feet, we strode over a glass floor. Murky black waters churned underneath the thick glass. As I approached a chair, an angler fish darted toward the surface, only to retreat again.

What else lurked down there?

And even more importantly, how was there water under the boat's third floor?

"You've collected many beautiful things," I said, unsure where to start.

Mimi's brows knitted together. "Natalya, you're not here to talk about my collecting habits. Spit it out."

I turned to her at the sound of my name. She meant business now. I told my former employer the entire tale from beginning to end. I gave every detail, no matter how small, from how I tracked the prints and got attacked that first night up until this moment, when I sat in a chair before her with a frost wolf's teeth marks festering in my leg. I also mentioned Farley was missing.

"I've come to believe Dayla has your whistle," I added in a whisper.

While I spoke, night servants glided into the room carrying small bowls. The enticing scent of a spiced punch with persimmons, ginger, and cinnamon filled the air. Her gray-skinned staff had patches of vivid green moss for hair and shiny obsidian flecks for eyes. They served each of us a small serving of punch. I didn't touch mine and continued my tale. The night demon nodded here and there, sipping her drink. When I finished, she didn't speak for the longest time.

I took my time to drink. The cool punch soothed my unsettled stomach while we waited.

Finally, she spoke. "I'd like to say I saw this coming, but I didn't. It's a shame when your kin would rather stab you in the back than fight you face to face."

The frightening demon I'd glimpsed days ago sagged forward in her seat. She stared past us, her features softening. She almost appeared human.

"She went to a lot of effort to make you leave this place," I forced myself to say.

"There would've been less bloodshed if she'd said something," Mimi said bitterly.

"But would you have listened?"

She slowly shook her head. "I was tired of her always having her way. I always needed her more than she needed me." The starlight in her hair brightened with her rising anger. "It was my turn to shine this time. It was my turn to feast on the night and moonlight."

I nodded with sympathy. "I've always wanted to be stronger too. But two people at odds can't stay that way forever. Someone must open themselves up and admit what they want and need without repercussions."

Mimi drew a deep breath. "Dayla didn't do that."

"No, she didn't." I swallowed deeply.

"She will use the whistle in the morning."

That made me stiffen. "She'll use it to call Cerberus and drive the goddess away?"

"She will do that and more," the night demon replied.

"Doesn't she know what will happen?" Aggie asked, clearly irked.

"Yes, but that doesn't matter to creatures like Dayla and me," Mimi explained. "Once that monster rampages north, killing anything that gets in the way of its order, my sister and I will still remain. The sun will rise and the moon will fall, but others won't be as lucky. Especially the people in South Toms River."

I slowly shook my head. Would have I been as wise with the whistle? A part of me believed I would've figured out a way to make it work. I could've summoned the hellhound in Sourland National Preserve.

"I must face my sister in the morning," she said.

"How?" I asked. "I thought you slept during the day."

"I do, but there's a span of time when I can manifest before the light drives me back to the barge. This won't be easy."

The night demon rubbed her chin with the back of her hand. "Over the last couple of months, Dayla has grown in strength as daytime has lengthened."

The frost giant's great power compared to the simpler night guards came to mind.

"While I distract her," Mimi said, "I'll need all of you to retrieve the whistle."

I tried to hide a laugh and failed. "Are you serious? It took every able-bodied adult in the pack, and two spellcasters, to take down the frost giant. Do you believe we can waltz past her to take the whistle?"

Mimi slowly licked her lips. "I'll be the one fighting her head-on. What you must do is what you do best: think quickly on your feet. Once you find the whistle, Farley should be nearby."

That sounded easier said than done.

"Do you know if she has more day guards like the frost giant?" Thorn asked.

"If I have night guards watching over the Midnight Barge," the night demon replied, "she'll have day guards, but they won't be as powerful as the frost giant. She used a lot of ingredients to craft *both* the giant and the wolf."

That news didn't make me feel any better.

Mimi continued, "Our battle will affect space and time, which will give you more time to find the whistle, but you can't dawdle. Once the sun fully rises, your doom will be sealed." She told us how she wanted things to unfold, but even I had doubts we'd succeed.

"I don't like any of this," I said. "There are innocent homes and business along the river."

"They will come to no harm. Our fight won't bleed into the human world." With that said, she stood and poured herself another serving of punch.

She added more to my cup, but I couldn't drink any more. Aggie gladly snatched my portion.

With our plans made, all we had left was small talk.

"Now that we know what to do," I said, "I gotta ask, why did you have the whistle out in the open for sale in the *first* place?"

Mimi rolled her eyes. "Some people are *smart* enough to do their research and not blow ancient whistles associated with monsters. And you can't tell me you've never met serious collectors at The Bends."

"Yeah, I'm one of them," I admitted.

She gave me a long, hard look to make her point. "I'd bet good money you've got at least one thing you've bought that you've never unwrapped or used." She folded her arms. "I'll wait."

Aggie giggled and Erica tried to hold back a laugh.

"Point made," I grumbled.

CHAPTER 24

While we waited for dawn, the night demon summoned her servants to help us get comfortable. A night guard brought Aggie and Erica blankets. Within minutes, Aggie collapsed into slumber. Erica tried to go to sleep, but eventually she got up and explored the artifacts in Mimi's chamber.

My mate refused to sleep. He'd finished his punch and stood guard in the corner.

To my surprise, a night servant with circular white coral for eyes and waist-length ferns for hair approached me with a red velvet-covered box. It perched next to me and opened the box to reveal an antique Victorian sewing box. I marveled at the pleated satin lining within and the delicate mother-of-pearl-handle tools. Spools of bright silver thread were nestled next to a pocketknife, tweezers, and a button-hook. How lovely. I almost touched them when the pale creature reached for my leg.

"What are you doing?" I whispered.

The night guard gestured to my wound and made sewing motions.

"You want to stitch it up?" I took a peek at the very much unsanitary-looking spool of silver thread with the needles poking out of its sides. "Do you have rubbing alcohol?"

That got me a questioning head tilt from the night guard.

"Nat, can you just let it do its work?" Erica asked. "Your leg looks really bad. We can get you a rabies shot later."

"Fine." I closed my eyes and dove into my happy place. Growth level nine achieved.

While the night servant prepared its materials, Thorn paced. I knew he wanted to storm into Dayla's domain and rescue his father, but now wasn't the time.

Minutes turned to hours. The throbbing pain in my leg lessened as the night servant's hands moved at a snail's pace to create perfectly spaced stitches. I should've relaxed, but the fear racing along my spine intensified. Would the Daylight Dame harm Farley while we waited? How I wished I could peel back the fog and tell my family to run and hide from what might come if Dayla blew the whistle and unleashed Cerberus in the town.

The clock ticked on until the time to move arrived at 6:31 a.m. We had five minutes until dawn.

Mademoiselle Midnight appeared before us. "Good to see almost everyone up." She threw a glance at Aggie.

Erica shook Aggie's shoulder, and my bestie rubbed her eyes. From past experience, she got up quickly, bad morning breath and all.

The night demon assessed her servant's handiwork on my leg. "Looks good. The moonlight thread will reduce swelling and counteract the wolf's frostbite."

I shifted in my chair to see the night servant had finished its work. So, the thread was moonlight, huh? The silver thread in my skin glinted with an unnatural shine.

"Bring her goblin blade that you retrieved from the wolf's car," Mimi said.

Another night servant arrived with my goblin blade on a silver plate. The weapon appeared to hover in midair.

"Thank you," I said softly, not wanting to imagine the night servants breaking into the SUV. "Will everyone else need weapons?"

"The strength of the pack will have to suffice," she said.

With our final preparations completed, we left Mimi's private quarters. As we descended the stairs to the Main Deck, I tried to clamp down on my agitation. This was a fight like any other.

Of course, it didn't help when my friends complained.

"I thought I was done with all this magic mess," Aggie said dryly.

"Once you ride the merry-go-round," Erica said with a snort, "you never seem to get off again."

I reminded everyone of the plan. "Once the sun rises, we must be inside the mart to rescue Farley and retrieve the whistle."

"What if we don't make it?" Thorn asked.

"We have to make it," I said firmly. "The night demon said the switch from night to day will occur and the sun will restore Dayla to full strength. We must use the battle to our advantage and sneak inside."

Everyone nodded.

"Last night, Mimi said we should keep our human forms. I don't like that idea," Aggie said.

We picked up the pace to disembark from the barge. Hints of the sunrise lightened the horizon from blue-black to light purple.

I sighed. "We're weaker in our human forms, but hopefully, it's not as simple as us needing opposable thumbs."

That got me an eye roll from Aggie and Erica. Damn, those two had become quite the pair.

"Hey, Timekeeper," Aggie said to me. "How much time left?"

I glanced at my watch. "Less than a minute. Be ready to move, everyone."

We waited, our breaths quickened, as the Toms River next to the barge churned and writhed. A dark purple light broke through the murkiness and blossomed. Thorn stumbled back. The rest of us froze. White tendrils of hair surfaced first as a creature emerged and rose higher. Ten feet became twenty, then fifty. A woman dressed in golden armor with a honey-brown face and high cheekbones floated over the river as miles of translucent white ribbon circled her. Smoke and fog swirled at her feet. She inclined her head to shake off river branches from the spiked golden crown on her curly chartreuse hair.

"What is that?" Thorn asked.

"I think that's Mademoiselle Midnight's true form," Aggie croaked.

I pushed a gaping Erica forward. Time wasn't on our side.

To the east, the horizon bled crimson streaks instead of brightening with the oncoming sun. Those streaks shot up to the heavens, then dipped to converge downriver from the night demon. At the convergent point, a large ruby red cloud formed. Lightning and bursts of fire stretched and contracted in the cloud as massive, pale fingers reached outward. First the hand, then a forearm covered in a silver vambrace emerged. More of the night demon's adversary slipped out until a woman stepped barefoot onto the surface of the water. She didn't sink. The redheaded giant wore a white tunic and pants that pulsed with an unnatural light. The undulating cloud behind her rose until it drifted to sit on top of her head. A snarl formed on the Daylight Dame's face.

I kept looking over my shoulder at the awesome sight of

the two demon sisters, but as my watch hit 6:35 a.m., I pushed the others to circle around to the front of the ceramic mart.

Time to work.

"They could crush us like bugs," Aggie said.

"Stop looking!" Erica barked.

The fight between the demons was nothing more than a distraction at this point. I took point and broke into a run. Before we could make it to the front door, a few stone statues in the front of the store twitched.

The day guards had woken up.

Lawn gnomes, fawns, and two stone dragons jerked and ambled their way toward us. Even a four-foot-high pagoda wobbled and advanced.

The goblin blade vibrated in my hands as the weapon lengthened into a sickle with a humming black quartz blade. I advanced first at the family of lawn gnomes, swinging hard. "I'll hold them off while you get to the door."

The sickle smoothly sliced off the lawn gnomes' hats.

"Not a chance." Thorn picked up the nearest urn and hurled it at a fawn. The baby deer sidestepped the shot, only to double back. Aggie darted past the ornamental stone figures to reach the pile of marble. With a glint in her light blue eyes, she threw the blocks with a quarterback's precision at our attackers.

A thunderous sonic boom shook the ground and sent us sprawling. I glanced over the top of the stone outlet to see Mademoiselle Midnight's ribbon snake out to strike the Daylight Dame's vambraces. The day demon roared and snatched the ribbon. The massive white strip of fabric wrapped about Dayla's hands, cutting deep, but Dayla struck back and yanked backward, drawing her sister in close for a head butt.

Another boom from the demon's blow hammered my skull and left my ears ringing.

"Nat!" Aggie yelled. "Keep your head in the game."

I snapped my attention back to the mart doorway. The clock continued to tick, tick, tick.

We didn't have much time to get inside before the switch occurred. Erica took out one dragon, flinging it hard to the cement. The other stone dragon jumped on Thorn's back, but he grasped it with a growl and bashed it to bits on the ground.

With our enemies out of the way, we rushed to the door. I wrenched it open and the others followed. Once we got into the store's cool interior, I paused.

Something wasn't right.

Pleasant retail-store Muzak played from the speakers overhead, but the familiar aisles had shifted. I couldn't see directly to the back office. We could only go either left or right.

"What's wrong?" Aggie tugged at me as the ground rumbled again. "Why are we waiting? How much time until sunrise?"

We should've run out of time by now, but a quick check revealed we still had a minute left.

"Our battle will affect space and time, which will give you more time to find the whistle, but you can't dawdle," the night demon had said.

But how much time did we *really* have in this place?

"I say we go left," Thorn grunted.

"Just give me a moment," I snapped. "This might be a trap."

The one thing I did know was how everything had been placed before. I knew where every cup, saucer, and God-awful dish sat. If Dayla had scrambled the room, she could only rearrange it so many ways.

"Follow me." I darted to the right, taking note that the shelves with garish purple, pink, and puke-green mugs were in the front now, so that meant the shelves with the planters were elsewhere. My mind zipped and pinged as if the room were a Rubik's Cube waiting to be solved. By the time we emerged at the end of the maze, we'd found the back wall with two doors.

"Not another puzzle. Which one?" Erica whispered.

"I know my work sites," I said dryly. "Left for day. Right for the night."

We came to the closed door on the left side, and I couldn't contain my laugh as I turned the doorknob. "Opposable thumbs for the win."

I expected us to find a small back office and Farley sitting there, but a set of stairs led upward to light. I hesitated at the first step, but Farley's faint scent drew us to race upward.

"We're almost there," I shouted.

Suddenly, the whole stairwell shook. We were flung into the air before we tumbled down, flopping and falling on each other.

"Keep moving." My battle cry didn't sound as strong, but everyone regrouped, helping each other to reach the door. At the top, we entered a room bathed in white, with desks, chairs, and computers. Instead of a roof over our heads, the open sky with a massive sun loomed.

We'd reached the day demon's private domain.

Twenty seconds left, according to my watch.

On the other side of the room, we spotted an unconscious Farley sprawled on the floor. Right next to him on a pedestal lay the whistle, nestled between the pages of an opened paperback.

We darted across the expansive room, veering around the desks and chairs. Ten seconds left.

Thorn scooped up Farley while I reached for the whistle.

Before I could touch it, the room went from stark white to red.

Time's up.

The whistle sparkled, then burst into flames.

"Oh, c'mon," Aggie snapped.

I tried to grasp the burning whistle but screamed as the flames scorched my palm. I prepared myself to withstand the pain and do what had to be done—until I remembered what I had in my pocket. I slipped my hand inside and withdrew the jade beads. Without thinking, I swallowed every single one of them.

Bottoms up.

Then I grasped the whistle.

Sparks burst in my belly, and the sensation spread like fire ants nipping at my limbs. The whistle in my hand grew whiter and whiter with heat, but since I felt no pain, I held tight.

All around us, red desks turned to ash and the walls crumbled. Thorn held Farley close as we escaped from the office, racing down the steps to hurry through the doorway into the ceramic mart.

When we finally rushed out the left side back office door, we came to a halt in front of a store with wide-eyed early-morning customers.

CHAPTER 25

Amiddle-aged woman pushing a mini-cart, along with a couple in matching denim outfits, stared at us as if we'd fallen from the sky. A woman holding a small child on her hip glanced at the others.

A couple of tense seconds passed before Erica cried, "His dad collapsed in the office. Someone call 911!"

Shouting out those three numbers had a profound effect on humans. The middle-aged woman rushed to us while Thorn laid Farley on the floor. The couple in the bedazzled denim outfits coordinated calling for medical assistance. And the mother gave us a small blanket out of her diaper bag to prop up Farley's head.

"He's rather pale," Denim Guy said. "I bet it's that awful heat outside."

If only he knew. At least Farley's breath was steady and my father-in-law had a strong heartbeat. Hopefully, he'd wake up soon with a hell of a hangover.

While everyone fussed over him, I scanned through the store for the demons. The whistle weighed heavy in my palm with hints of heat.

"I'm going outside to wait for the ambulance," I told the others.

The humans nodded. Thorn stayed behind to maintain the act while Erica, Aggie, and I left the store.

"Do you think they're still fighting outside?" Aggie asked.

"I'd hate to have riverfront property right now," I replied. "'Cause I wouldn't want to be in the middle of that."

"I wouldn't want to own a boat on the marina, either," Erica added.

We stepped out carefully into the humid July air. More Sunday morning shoppers pulled into the quiet parking lot. Other customers browsed through the outdoor merchandise. Not a single ornament or stone appeared broken or overturned.

It was as if we hadn't fought the day guards.

I hurried around the mart to investigate the riverside. A pair of robins chirped from a nearby tree as the wind blew a breeze off the river. A family of five on a pontoon boat laughed and prepared for a pleasant Sunday outing on the river.

The Midnight Barge and the wrecked riverside had vanished, leaving the scene disturbingly tranquil.

So where had the demons gone?

"There you are, Niema," came a soft voice behind us.

We turned sharply to find Mademoiselle Midnight lounging under a black umbrella. She'd returned to the form I'd always seen her in, but her skin was far more translucent. Smokier. I thought she had to sleep during the day, but there she was.

The night demon gave me the smile of a proud mother. "I thought you'd fail, but look at you! You're as clever as the goblin claimed. Is Farley well?"

"Yeah, he's unconscious but stable."

She nodded and took a sip from a teacup with sludgy water. Ew.

"Where is your sister?" I asked. "Dayla's not in the shop."

Mimi pursed her lips and slowly put down the cup. "After we fought, she packed up and left."

I sighed. "I'm sorry about that. We can't always come to terms with our family when they have wronged us."

"No, we can't. And we'll always have our little spats now and then. This was nothing compared to the one time we melted a polar ice cap and started a tsunami in the Arctic." She clucked her tongue and shook her head.

"What about the store?" Erica asked.

"Humans will manage it during the day until I close at the end of the week." Mimi stared out to the water. "How I wished I could've stayed and made a tidy profit, but unfortunately, my sister and I are a knot. The knot will tighten up now and then, but we will always be one."

So the demons planned to leave? Maybe it was for the best. Having all those dangerous artifacts nearby would tempt the wrong people again.

"Am I free from our bargain, then?" I asked.

She smiled sweetly. "You will be once you return my property."

I considered tossing it to her, but instead, I tried to place it in her hand. The whistle slipped through her hand as if her flesh wasn't whole.

"Damn, all that fighting—and that stupid sun," she said.

I left the whistle at her feet and backed up.

"I also have the beads from the necklace," I added, "but I had to swallow them to touch the whistle."

Mimi's face scrunched up. Yeah, she'd have to get those back the old-fashioned way.

"I'm in no hurry to get those," she said with a grimace.

"And, well, I don't know if they'll *resurface* or become something else altogether."

Now that made my stomach quake. What did she mean by that?

The umbrella covering Mimi fluttered, turning from black to gray.

The night demon sighed. "It's time for me to rest. When I'm settled down, I'll send you an address for what's left of the bracelet. Be sure to…clean it thoroughly."

Before I could say goodbye, the night demon, her tea setting, and Cerberus's whistle flitted away like the last puffs of smoke from a dying fire.

~

An ambulance arrived and the paramedics were shocked to see their patient wake up with a curse and a curt "no thanks." Farley rose to his feet, dusted himself off, and marched out the door.

My poor mate was left apologizing profusely to everyone.

I didn't bother. Farley wasn't sorry for peppering fucks all over the place.

With Farley up and about, everyone left the mart, with Erica and Aggie returning home while we drove to the cottage.

"Those damn humans will poke and prod you until you're nothing more than a pincushion," Farley complained during the drive. "They don't know squat. Them demons just drained me a bit, that's all."

"At least you could've been nice about it," Thorn said, sounding quite tired, but relieved his dad was well.

Once we reached the turnoff to the cottage, Farley grunted from the back seat. "Where we are going?"

"Home," I said.

"I thought I had a new home now. Isn't Will already living there?"

Thorn's gaze briefly connected with mine. What did he mean?

My mate pulled the SUV over to the side of the road.

"As I was driving out of Double Trouble to meet the day demon," Farley said, "I had time to think about someone other than myself. I was a part of the pack again. Running. Fighting." He stared out the window into the woods. "I've carried a lot of crap around, and I shouldn't be taking a shit in someone else's backyard. I need to go my own way."

Then he added, "Also, after you made me *give* away my beer, I don't think I need that kind of nonsense."

My heart warmed at his words, even if they were a bit crass.

"Are you sure you don't want to stay and share your beers with the clurichaun?" Thorn replied with a wide smile.

"I'll pass." Farley motioned for us to get going.

No one spoke during the entire trip to my former home—now Farley's. Soon enough, we arrived and Farley made himself comfortable on the La-Z-Boy. He propped his feet up and grabbed the TV remote.

Thorn smiled again at his crusty sire's antics and prepared to leave, but I lingered to say something that had nibbled at me from the moment we arrived at the mart last night.

"Farley, there's something I gotta know," I said. "How did you get into the day demon's store?"

That got me a rare smile from Farley. "I'm smart, girl."

"No, really."

He sighed. "I've been alive for a long time, and I've learned a thing or two about those shifty demons. They *love* a good deal, and if you've made one before, the others are more open to hearing from you."

The former pack leader turned the TV turned on, effectively dismissing us.

Thorn glanced at me, and we probably had the same question: what deal had he made in the past?

We wouldn't get the answer today, but someday I'd pry it out of him.

As we left, my gaze lingered on the room that once served as my sanctuary. My former furniture still sat in the same spot, but the containers with my holiday cheer had been relocated to the home I shared with my mate. The kitchen had plenty of healthy food, and the bedroom linens were fresh and ready for Farley to slumber like a pup tonight. Farley had yet to touch the carving kit or the pieces of black walnut, but the tools would be waiting if inspiration struck him.

This place was finally a home again.

"I'll come by later and check on you," Thorn said.

"Goodbye, Farley," I added.

As we walked out, I faintly heard Farley say, "Be careful, you two."

I paused on the stoop, then kept going when Thorn took my hand. The warmth from his palm seeped into me, bringing a cheesy grin to my face. We got into the car, him in the driver's seat and me on the passenger side. I waited for us to pull away, but he rolled down the window and looked at the cottage instead.

"I still can't believe he moved in," Thorn whispered.

"Neither can I."

"Do you think he won't need us if we go on that Maine trip?"

I chuckled. "He's a grown man. If he needs anything, he's

got Will. And my family can give him more company than he'll *ever* want."

With our spirits lifted, we returned home. Settling in after everything that had happened should've been easier, but as Thorn left to make a grocery run, I stood in the living room and a dark feeling slithered through my chest. It was remorse.

I stared out my window to the beds of golden sunflowers and fragrant chrysanthemums I'd replanted, and I tried to release the regret, but the feeling lingered. My remorse slipped around my neck like an adversary's impending attack, pressed against my windpipe, and jerked upward.

You could've ended what was to come, my heart whispered. *You had the whistle right there in your hand.*

I staggered to the sofa and rested my head against pillows that smelled like violet fabric softener. The room was cool and the house silent, but the past I'd buried resurfaced with vivid clarity. For while the goddess Diana had chained me to that spot in Sourland Natural Preserve, she used the wind, the sun, and the rain to reveal promises and prophecies.

I will return for you, Wolf, the wind said.

No matter how often the golden sun rises and falls, you once belonged to me, the sun said.

You know the weight of the leash connecting you to me, and soon enough, I will yank the chain. And you will kneel. You will beg for the scraps I feed my animals, the moon said. *Unless you wish to run from me, and I* hope *you do.*

The goddess had added, *For our struggle will become the Hunt of the Ages. A feast for my soul. And at the conclusion of that Endless Night, you will surrender and be mine forevermore.*

I blew out a deep breath and tried to not shake.

"Sister Wolf still has work to do," Mevelyn had said. I forced myself to get up and fetch the fly-fishing lure Mevelyn had

crafted for me. The handcrafted wooden minnow had exquisite detail from its head down to its tail. I ran my fingers along the tiny gift, its bumps and ridges a reminder of her sacrifice.

My fight had only just begun.

THE END

COVETED

Prequel
Novella
0.5

Book
1

Book
2

Novella
2.5

Book
3

Short Story
Collection

Prequel feat.
Aggie
McClure

VALKYRIE
RISING
PRESS

ABOUT THE AUTHOR

Shawntelle Madison is a Web developer who loves to weave words as well as code. She'd be reluctant to admit it, but if pressed, she'd say that she covets and collects source code. After losing her first summer job detasseling corn, Madison performed various jobs, from fast-food clerk to grunt programmer to university webmaster. Writing eccentric characters is her favorite job of all. On any given day when she's not surgically attached to her computer, she can be found watching cheesy horror movies or the latest action-packed anime. Shawntelle Madison lives in Missouri with her husband and children.